JUDGMENT DAY

JUDGMENT DAY

by

David Whitehead

Dales Large Print Books
Long Preston, North Yorkshire,
BD23 4ND, England.

British Library Cataloguing in Publication Data.

Whitehead, David
    Judgment day.

    A catalogue record of this book is
    available from the British Library

    ISBN   978-1-84262-778-5 pbk

First published in Great Britain in 1994 by Robert Hale Limited

Copyright © David Whitehead 1994

Cover illustration © Michael Thomas

The right of David Whitehead to be identified as the author of this work has been asserted by him in accordance with the Copyright, Designs and Patents Act, 1988

Published in Large Print 2011 by arrangement with David Whitehead

Dales Large Print is an imprint of Library Magna Books Ltd.

Printed and bound in Great Britain by
T.J. (International) Ltd., Cornwall, PL28 8RW

For Crispin Jackson
– positively my favourite editor

ONE

They jumped him about thirty seconds after he left the hotel.

He never stood a chance.

It had always been his custom to take an unhurried, relaxing stroll after supper, no matter where he might be. It was a habit that had developed over the sixty-seven years of his life, and tonight was no different.

Until, that was, they were upon him.

It wasn't even seven o'clock in the evening, but already the streets were deserted. Winter was starting to squeeze the Wyoming foothill country with a bitter hand, bringing early darkness and strong, biting winds, and in the low clouds above, the threat of snow.

Most folks with any sense were snugged up indoors.

But not the old man.

And not his attackers.

He came out onto the porch, wrapped in a heavy greatcoat and scarf, his muley hat tugged low over white grey hair and the town reflected in his small round spectacles. He paused for a moment, shivering at the prospect of another high-country winter, then turned left, hands stuffed deep in his pockets, shoulders hunched against the cold blow, head down, just thinking, and almost before he knew it – they were there.

There were two of them. Where they sprang from, he would never know. But in the very same instant that he realised he was no longer alone, they had him.

They crowded in on him, hands grasping his arms, fingers digging through his clothes, and shoved him sideways so that he stumbled into a darkened, garbage-stinking alley beside the hotel.

His hat flew off and bounced against the hardpan. As his assailants followed him into the darkness, one of them flattened it underfoot.

More angry than alarmed – but alarmed as well – the old man blinked at the two men. They were little more than dark, silent shadows, buttoned to the throat in sheep-skin jackets, wide-brimmed hats pulled down at the front, the barest glimmer of the swaying streetlights showing on the cold iron of their sidearms.

At last he found his voice and stammered, 'Now s-see here…'

One of them struck out then, backhanding his face sideways, and his glasses flew off, sparkled for a moment in midair, then fell among the garbage.

Outrage boiled to the surface. 'What the…! You men–'

But before he could say more, his attackers crowded in on him again and threw him up against the brick wall, and he struck it hard with a groan and a grimace.

'Who … who are you?' he asked, more alarmed than anything else now, his vision just a blur.

They made no reply, and he found their

silence even more unnerving.

Gamely he pushed away from the wall and tried to make a break for it, but one of them grabbed him by the front of his greatcoat and swung him around, and as the coat came open, the buttons flew off and went spinning into the darkness.

The same faceless man hit him in the stomach and he doubled over, wanting to vomit. He heard them moving in, their heavy breathing as they dragged him back up and hit him again. Then, as he fell and they started to kick him, he heard the rasp and rustle of their clothing, the little, under-the-breath profanities they muttered as they went to work on him.

The pain grew so intense that he no longer bothered with such minutiae after that. He opened his mouth, and this time all trace of his earlier indignation was gone. 'Please...' he husked. 'Please ... take my wallet... H-here ... take it all...'

But they paid him no mind. Perhaps they didn't hear him. Perhaps they enjoyed hurting him so much that robbery was only a secondary consideration. Whichever it was, the pain continued, a kick here, a stomp there, dragging him up, slapping him around, more punches to the face and body.

Even in his confusion, he knew he was lucky. His thick clothes offered some protection against it all, absorbing much of the force. But still he hurt. He hurt worse than he thought it was possible for a man *to* hurt.

Again he tried to reason with them. 'Please … you don't … have to … do this…'

But again they ignored him.

Then, a lifetime later, one of them bent down and slapped him a few times, but more gently, to drag him back from unconsciousness and get his attention.

He tried to focus on the man. Without his spectacles it was impossible. All he could see was an indistinct, flesh-coloured oval, and darker pits where the eyes, nose and mouth should be.

A hand grabbed his blood-flecked chin and the blurry face pushed closer, so that the old man could feel the whisper of his fetid breath. 'Go home, old man,' a voice hissed, enunciating every word so that there would be no possible misunderstanding. 'You hear me? *Go – home.*'

Addled by the beating, the old man said, 'What? I don't understand…'

'It's simple. Turn around. Forget all about Little Cody. You're not wanted there. You go back where you come from an' you'll go on livin'. Keep a-comin' an' God help me, we'll kill you.'

The old man, hugging himself now, looked up at him, just discerning the vapour-cloud steaming around his mouth, and said, 'Please…'

But the other man was all through talking. He struck the old man again, an open-handed slap that pushed him sideways into the frozen mud and refuse that had been piled at the foot of the wall.

'They's a stage out of here tomorrow mornin',' he said. 'Be on it.'

Then he drew his foot back to deliver one

final kick.

Before he could launch it, however, a voice down at the street-end of the alley suddenly bellowed, *'Hey, you there!'*

The old man's aggressors turned to face the speaker. Outlined against the gas street-lights stood two men, both tall and lean-looking even though they too were bundled up against the chill. As one, the bully-boys twisted around and started running for the other end of the alley.

'Hold it!' cried one of the men who had interrupted the beating.

But of course, they had no intention of holding it, not now that they'd been dis-covered.

In his haste to get away, one of the bully-boys stumbled over an old chair-frame and went sprawling headlong onto the ground. Frantically he clawed his way back to his feet and kicked the obstruction free. Glancing over his shoulder, he got a quick glimpse of the newcomers, charging into the alley now, still yelling out for them to stop, and desperately his hand dropped to the Colt at his hip.

His buddy bawled, *'Come on!'*

But now that the gun was in his hand, he felt more like fighting than fleeing, so he shoved the weapon out to arm's length, thumbed back the hammer and loosed off a shot, and orange flame stabbed back at their would-be pursuers.

The bullet flew a little to the left and hit the side of the hotel. It punched a handful of stone chips out into the air and then whined off into the distance, spent and mis-shapen.

Somewhere far off, dogs started yapping and squealing, either afraid or excited. The two men at the street-end of the alley ducked low, realising that the hissing, high-mounted lamps made them prime targets, then threw themselves further into the alley and up against the wall, where they blended with all the other shadows.

A second later another stab of flame accompanied a gunshot, but this time it was one of the newcomers who was doing the shooting.

Down on his side, the old man tried to sit up, but when every muscle in his body started throbbing, he groaned and curled into a ball instead. He heard the sound of men running toward him – his saviours, he thought dimly. Another gunblast roared overhead, one last, parting shot from the men who had meant, and dealt, him harm.

A voice carried to him on the chilly wind, low, grim, Texan. 'Look after him, Matt. I'm goin' after 'em.'

And a response: 'All right. But watch yourself.'

He felt a hand on his arm, and cracked his eyes open. He saw the silhouette of a young man crouching over him. The silhouette – *Matt,* his companion had called him – said, 'You all right, mister?'

The old man thought about it for a moment, analysing the question. His normally agile mind had been slowed down and jumbled up by the beating. Finally he whispered, 'I … I think so. But … my spectacles… I can't see a thing without…'

'All right, all right. I'll find your glasses for you in a minute. Where'd you lose 'em?'

The old man gestured vaguely toward the street-end of the alley.

Matt said. 'They rob you?'

'N-no.'

'Guess we happened along just in time, then.'

The old man frowned, at last realising that what had just happened here had nothing to do with robbery. He shivered and Matt said again, 'You *sure* you're all right?'

'Just … just cold, that's all.'

'Well, when my partner comes back, we'll get you inside. You staying at the hotel?'

'Yes.'

'So're we.'

'Your, uh … partner. He's … gone after them?'

'Uh-huh.'

'C-call him back… Please. I don't want anyone … taking risks … on my behalf…'

'It's all right, mister. Sam knows what he's doing.'

'Sam?'

'Sam Judge. My partner.'

The old man said the name again, in his head. It sounded familiar to him, although he couldn't place it immediately. He sighed and closed his eyes against another wave of nausea, then thought to introduce himself. 'I'm M-Moffat,' he croaked tiredly. 'Lewis … Moffat. If you hadn't … come along when you did, Mr…?'

Matt patted him gently on the shoulder. 'Matt Dury, sir,' he replied. 'You just rest quietly a minute.'

They heard sounds coming from the far end of the alley just then and turned that way, the old man squinting and making frustrated little mutterings at not being able to see too well. Beside him, Matt called out, 'Sam?'

A second later a voice came to them out of the darkness. 'Yeah, it's me. I'm comin' in.'

Sam strode back towards them, gun still in hand, breathing hard from the chase. When he was near enough, Matt said,

'They get away?'

'They got away.' Sam crouched and asked the old man how he felt, and the old man, Lewis Moffat, said he was feeling better now that it was all over.

'You feel chipper enough to move?'

He nodded. 'If … if it means getting in … out of the c-cold.'

Sam cracked him a lopsided smile. 'Come on then, mister, let's get you on your feet. Matt, better go see if you can find a doctor.'

The old man said, 'Ah, there's no need for–'

'Looks to me like there's *every* need, friend. Them sumbitches beat you up pretty thorough. Won't do no harm to let a sawbones check you over.'

Matt said, 'Can you manage on your own?'

'Sure.'

With a nod, Matt straightened up, turned away and started off back up the alley. His partner watched him go, then stuffed his heavy Remington .44 away and helped the old man to his feet, waiting a moment for the old man's swimming head to clear a bit.

At last, supporting him with one arm around his waist, he helped the old man up the alley and back out onto the windy street.

As soon as they pushed into the hotel and the man and the woman who were waiting expectantly in front of the reception desk got a good look at the old man's puffed and bloody face, the woman's mouth turned into a round tunnel of surprise and the man, Todd Jackson, who owned the place, said, 'Good heavens, judge! What happened? We heard what sounded like a couple of shots being fired–'

He hurried over and helped the old man to a chair, into which he flopped gratefully. The lobby was bright and rather more opulent than such a small, out-of-the-way town warranted. A glass-paned door in the facing wall led through to the restaurant. A similar door in the right-hand wall opened into the bar. A few guests or patrons had gathered in both doorways, a couple more on the staircase that wound up to the first, second and third floors, doubtless drawn by the gunfire and anxious to find out what had been going on.

At first, Sam thought that Todd Jackson had been addressing him, Judge being his surname. But as he opened his mouth to reply, the hotelier brushed straight past him and knelt at the old man's side.

For his part, the old man waved one hand in a little circular motion, trying to make light of what had occurred. 'I was ... attacked...' he murmured.

Jackson said over his shoulder, 'Marge – get a drink for the judge. Quick now!'

'My partner's gone for a doctor,' Sam said quietly.

Jackson looked up at him. He had oily fair hair and he was in his late thirties, although he didn't look it. 'Thank you. Did you see what happened?'

'Not the whole of it. Me an' my partner went down to Buckman's Livery to check on our horses. On the way back, we heard a commotion comin' from that alleyway out yonder. When we took a closer look, we saw two fellers beatin' the old man up. Minute we tried to brace 'em, they lit out.'

'So it was you who fired the shots?'

'Well, I kinda what you might call *retaliated*. That's to say, they started shootin' first.'

'Did you get them?'

'No.'

'Too bad.'

Marge brought a glass of brown whiskey and together she and the hotelier got some of it into the old man. Sam saw that the old man had a round, lined face with brown eyes and a button nose. His white-grey hair was mussed up and thinning. Sam guessed he usually scraped it across his now-exposed pink pate in an attempt to make it look more than what it actually was. Colour came back into his loose cheeks as the whiskey went to work on him, but when some of the raw spirit trickled into his split lip, he gave a wince and a shudder and Sam noticed a set of store-bought teeth sitting uneasily inside his mouth.

His own expression hardened as he took in the full extent of the old man's injuries. The old man's face looked like a bag full of river rocks. His right eye was puffed half shut. His bottom lip was swollen to twice its normal size. His cheeks were either grazed or purple with bruises. And blood from maybe a dozen little splits in the skin was drying to a dull red crust.

'Come on, judge, let's get you into my office,' said Jackson. He reached down and helped the old man up, and Sam stood back to allow him and the woman to guide him across the lobby and through a door behind the desk.

Around them, the other guests went back to their rooms or meals or drinks, muttering to each other in scandalised tones about what had happened. Outside, the wind picked up and moaned on around the side of the building, making the windows creak in their frames. Sam shivered and began to unbutton his brown wool jacket. He was a tall man, six feet two or three, and his long legs and lean, flat-bellied build served only to make him look even taller.

Taking off his round-crowned, buff-coloured Stetson, he ran the splayed fingers of his right hand through his fine, black-mixing-to-grey hair. His hand appeared slightly odd to anyone seeing it for the first time, because it was missing the little finger.

With nothing more to occupy him here, he decided to repair to the bar and await the arrival of his partner. Crossing the lobby, he pushed into a small, comfortable and – mercifully – well-heated bar-room and ordered a whiskey, then chose a spot from which he could see the lobby through the ornate glass door, and fished a cigar from his shirt pocket. They were foul things, a fact confirmed by their knock-down, three-for-a-dime price, but he had grown accustomed to them over the years and now, as he struck a phosphor and lit up, he allowed his thoughts to turn back to the recent conflict.

About ten minutes later he saw his partner

shoulder into the lobby with a tall, very dark man and a few wispy flakes of snow trailing him. The dark man's black leather bag identified him clearly as a doctor. Almost at once they were met by Todd Jackson, and there was a brief exchange between them. Just before the doctor went through to see to the old man, Sam saw Matt hold something out for him to take along with him – the old man's glasses.

Matt joined him a moment later, rubbing his cold hands together as he caught the bartender's eye and asked for a beer. A tall, straight-backed man down at the other end of the bar cleared his throat to attract their attention and said, 'Those drinks are on me, Sid. Appears these two gentlemen are bona fide heroes.'

Sam and his companion raised their glasses to him, and Sam said, 'Obliged to you, friend.'

Sam was about two years past his mid-forties, with a lean, weatherbeaten, slightly mournful face and gentle grey eyes. He was a mostly quiet man, sometimes moody, often short on patience, and he tended to hide a surprisingly sensitive nature beneath a bluff, tough exterior.

Matt was about half Sam's age and, at six feet even, only marginally shorter. He shared a similar kind of build to his companion and the same sort of long, vaguely melancholy face, but Matt was undeniably more handsome than Sam had ever been, with thick, curly black hair, deep, curiously young-old eyes the colour of gunmetal and a square, firm jaw pitted by a dimple.

'Well,' said Matt, raising his glass to his lips. 'I guess that was one way to liven up a dull evening.'

'You *could* say that.'

'How was the old man when you fetched him in?'

Sam shrugged. 'Not too good. But he looks like a tough old bird.' As an afterthought he added, 'He's a judge.'

Matt frowned. 'Can't be. He told me his name was Moffat.'

'I don't mean a *Judge*. I mean a *judge*. A real-live, gavel-bangin' sentence-passer.'

Matt narrowed his gaze at him. 'Is that supposed to mean something?'

Sam drained his glass, beginning to warm through at last. 'I don't know. I guess not.'

'But…?'

'What do you mean, "but"?'

'Aw, come on, Sam. You got something on your mind. I know all the signs. You've started smoking those God-awful cheroots again, for a start.'

Sam smiled and shook his head. 'Aw, pay me no mind, boy. After a while, it gets so you start lookin' too deep into just 'bout everythin',' he remarked. Then, signalling that the subject was closed, he said, 'Hungry?'

'Uh-huh.'

'Come on, then. Let's go get somethin' to eat.'

It was as they were finishing up with a pot of good hot coffee half an hour later that a blocky man of average height came into the restaurant and, spying them, wound between all the other tables to reach them. By that time the Texans had the room almost to themselves, the other diners having drifted out in twos and threes as the evening grew older.

Now they watched the newcomer skirt around all the furniture and come to a halt beside them, twisting his damp hat in his hands. He was in his forties, with longish, straw-coloured hair fringing a shining dome and a darker, thicker moustache adorning his upper lip. He introduced himself as George Mitchell, the town constable, then said, 'Mind if I have a word with you fellers about that robbery you helped to foil?'

Sam shrugged. 'Sure. Have a seat, Mitchell. Coffee?'

Mitchell nodded gratefully. 'Thanks. It's cold as a witch's tit out there tonight.'

'Still snowing?' asked Matt.

'Not so's you'd notice, but we'll get it tomorrow, nothing surer.'

The plain-faced woman who waited at table had seen the constable come in and as soon as Sam raised a hand to her, she fetched another cup. As Sam poured coffee for him, he said, 'How's the old man?'

'Judge Moffat?' The constable shook his head. 'They beat him bad, I can tell you. But old Lew Moffat, he's stronger'n snakehead whiskey. He took a mess of cuts and contusions, and Doc Wellman thinks he might have cracked a bone in his left wrist when he fell over. But other'n that, he'll be all right. I just come from talking with him. He asked me to thank you for helping him out like you did.'

The lawman's lively hazel eyes narrowed on Matt's plate. 'Say, you leaving that leg o'chicken there, son?'

'Uh-huh.'

'Then pass me your plate. I hate to see food go to waste, and in any case, I haven't had any supper yet, thanks to this business.'

As Matt passed the plate to him, the constable said, 'You mind telling me what happened out there?'

They didn't mind at all. Sam told it in a

few sentences. It didn't take long.

At the end of it, Mitchell pushed Matt's plate away from him, finished chewing and then asked, 'So you fellers didn't get much of a look at the men who did the beating?'

'Not a good one. They was hardly more'n a couple of shadows to us,' Sam replied. 'I take it the judge didn't get a good look at 'em, either?'

'Naw. And once he lost his glasses...'

Sam nodded and dug out a couple of cigars, one of which he offered to the constable. 'This kind of thing happen around her often, Mitchell?' he asked as he produced a match, struck it and held it to the other man's smoke.

Once he had the cigar going, the constable shook his head. 'Hardly ever. That's why I'd like to get my hands on these fellers before they try it again.'

'You think they're local men?'

'I wouldn't think so. This is a decent, law-abiding community we got here. Sometimes we get copper miners come into town to see the elephant, but nothing like this.'

'Any newcomers in town lately?'

Mitchell smiled – no easy task when you were trying to smoke one of Sam's noxious weeds. 'Only you two,' he replied. 'By Christ, you ask a lot of questions, don't you, Judge?'

'Old habits die hard, I guess.'

'That's about what I was hoping you'd say,' Mitchell remarked softly.

It went quiet around the table now that they were finally getting down to cases. 'What does that mean?' asked Matt.

Mitchell looked at each of them in turn. Every so often the level of the light rose or fell as a stray draught slipped in through one of the windows and played with the flickering, hissing lamps that were fixed to the walls at regular intervals.

'I know all about you two,' he said. 'Oh, you might *think* you're anonymous, but you've earned yourselves quite a reputation these past couple of years, and your reputation travelled up this way a long time before you did. I've heard all about your exploits, Judge, first as a Texas Ranger, you an' Dury's paw, God rest him, then as a town-tamer. Way I hear it, you was like Earp, Hickok and Stoudenmire all rolled into one back then, and pure deadly hell with that there hogleg of yourn. That's why they took to calling you "The Pistol Prince", wasn't it? In them five-cent books Ned Buntline used to put out on you?'

'You don't want to believe everythin' you read in them yellow-jackets,' Sam replied sourly, chewing his cigar over to the corner of his mouth. 'Eddie Judson, he always did like to stretch the truth a little.'

Mitchell overlooked that. 'Then there's you, Dury. Seems like you're following in your old man's footsteps, tying up with Judge here. But it wasn't always like that, was it? I know you're pretty slick with them Tranters you carry in that fancy buscadero weapons belt. Also hear that you looked set to become a bit of a hellion till Judge showed you the error of your ways.'

Frowning now, Sam said, 'Is this leadin'

up to anythin', Mitchell, or are you jus' flappin' your gums for the exercise?'

The constable said, 'I'm trying to ask you a favour, and I'm hoping you'll oblige me out of professional courtesy. As one lawman to another, you might say.'

'Well, they's sure nothin' wrong with that – 'ceptin' for the fact that I don't pack a badge no more.'

'Man doesn't always need a badge to uphold the law,' Mitchell responded. 'Since you two've been on the drift together, you've built yourselves something of a reputation for stepping in when the law isn't up to the job, or where there ain't no law at all. Regulators, they're calling men like you nowadays.'

The Texans exchanged a look. Sure enough, Mitchell was right about that. Somehow or another, they had developed a talent for getting involved in other folks' trouble. That run-in with the Stovers in Nevada, for instance. Mixing it up with those renegade Apaches in the Arizona Territory. Tangling with Django Reilly down in Nebraska. Getting involved in the Tabosa Valley Sheep War. And now this business. Sometimes they got paid for it, other times they were motivated by nothing more than a simple – and some might say *simplistic* – sense of altruism.

Sam pondered the word Mitchell had used. *Regulators*. It sounded a whole sight better than *vigilantes*.

'What's the favour?' asked Matt.

'Judge Moffat,' Mitchell said quietly, setting his cigar aside – gratefully, Matt thought. 'He's got important business up in Little Cody. That's a mining town about three-score miles east of here, up in the Big-horns. I won't say too much about it, I don't think I should discuss it, somehow. But it's business that won't wait, so he's fixing to catch the stage out of here tomorrow morning.' He paused, then said, 'I'd like for you two to follow him and make sure he gets there in one piece.'

'What makes you think that he won't?' Matt asked.

'That business he got mixed up in tonight,' the constable explained. 'Oh, he didn't say anything. He wouldn't. That's not Lew Moffat's way. But if that really *was* an attempted robbery, then I'm a Chinese Jew.'

'How'd you figure that?'

Sam spoke up, answering for him. 'Because if you're gonna rob a man, you just do it an' then get the hell away from him. You don't stick around to beat him up as well. 'Sides which, any common thief'd high-tail was you to brace him. He wouldn't turn the whole she-bang into a shootin'-match.'

'That's it exactly,' the constable agreed.

Sam considered what Mitchell was asking of them. It was hardly the weather for a sixty-mile ride up into the ragged, timbered mountains that loomed over the town, especially if snow *was* on the way, as appeared likely. He and Matt had been figuring to ride south for the winter, down into New Mexico or Arizona. Being snowed-in up in the Bighorn Mountains just didn't hold the same appeal as resting up in warmer climes, somehow ... particularly if Mitchell's fears turned out to be groundless.

Still...

'We'd need to know a bit more than what you've already told us before we'd take on that kind of a chore,' he said at length.

Mitchell said, 'It's a delicate matter, Judge. But in a nutshell, Lew Moffat's heading up to Little Cody to try a man for murder. Well, whole *string* of murders, really. Now, that's got nothing to do with me. That all happened outside my bailiwick. But I got me a suspicion that certain ... parties ... up there would prefer it if the case never came to trial. I think that was them trying to scare the judge off tonight.'

Matt said, 'Is this just a hunch of yours, constable, or is there something more to it?'

'I'll be honest with you, Dury, I'm only going by what my instincts tell me. That and a passing acquaintance with some of the people involved.' He picked up the cigar again, inspected the dying tip, then put it down again. 'But I'm willing to back it up with hard cash, if that'll help sweeten the pot a bit. Deputies' wages for each of you, just for taking a ride up into the mountains, making sure the judge reaches Little Cody okay, and then coming straight back.'

Sam and Matt shared a glance. They were both thinking about the old man, Matt about how insistent he had been that they shouldn't risk themselves on his behalf even though he himself was hurting so bad, Sam about how thoroughly the judge's assailants had beaten him up.

After a moment Matt gave his companion an imperceptible nod, and Sam knew that they had more or less reached the same decision, and for much the same reasons. When it came down to it, they had nothing better to do, and the money would certainly come in handy. Besides which, the old man was entitled to some protection after what he'd already been through.

He said, 'All right, Mitchell. Looks like you just hired yourself a couple extra deputies.'

The constable positively beamed. 'Well, that's a weight off my mind, I can tell you.'

Sam gestured with the cigar. 'You know us regulators,' he said caustically. 'Always glad to be of service.'

Mitchell frowned. 'I got just one more question,' he said.

'What's that?'

The constable pointed to Sam's plate. 'You finished with that there steak, Judge? You have? Well, pass it over here. I'm famished, man, and–'

'We know, we know,' said Matt. 'You just hate to see good food go to waste.'

TWO

Judge Moffat himself caught up with them early the following morning, just as they came downstairs into the watery grey light of a cold new day and started across the lobby toward the restaurant, and breakfast.

He had been sitting in one of the button-studded chairs near the reception desk, his old leather bag resting beside him like a faithful brown puppy, obviously waiting for them to put in an appearance.

As he struggled to his feet, his movements were stiff and careful, occasionally drawing a flinch of discomfort from him, and although he was dressed for travel, he still looked pretty rough. The swelling about his right eye and in his bottom lip had gone down, and the marks over his cheekbones were starting to turn a sickly yellow colour at the edges, but he obviously wasn't fit enough yet to undertake the demanding trek up into the mountains. He was using a cane to steady himself, and his left hand was heavily bandaged.

'Mr Judge – Mr Dury,' he said with a nod, regarding them both through his flimsy-looking spectacles, one lens of which now sported a hairline crack. 'I fear I didn't get the chance to thank you properly for your, ah, assistance last night.'

The Texans shook hands with him, saying nothing of Constable Mitchell's visit with them the previous evening, nor the suspicions he had voiced during it. 'Forget it,' Sam replied. 'How're you feelin' this mornin'?'

The jurist put a brave face on it. 'Oh, much improved after a hot bath and a good night's sleep, thank you,' he answered. But the old man's eyes were tired and worried, and it was equally evident that in reality he hadn't slept a wink.

'Too bad you didn't get much of a look at

the men who knocked you around,' said Sam.

The judge's mouth thinned down. 'Yes,' he replied. He opened his mouth to speak again, but it seemed that he had a hard time deciding what he was going to say. In the end he just dropped his shoulders and said, 'Well, I must get down to the stage depot. I'm leaving town shortly.'

'Is that wise?'

'I'm afraid I have business elsewhere that simply cannot wait.'

'Can we give you a hand with your bag?'

'Thank you, no. You gentlemen have already done enough, and Mr Jackson has already offered to help me.'

'Take care then, judge,' said Matt.

The old man nodded. 'I will, Mr Dury. Goodbye to you, and thank you once again.'

They watched him turn, square his shoulders, set his reclaimed and reshaped muley hat atop his fine, sparse hair and then shuffle out into the street. If they'd been willing to believe that he needed protection last night, they were cast-iron sure of it this morning.

Matt clapped his partner on the arm and they went through to get some breakfast. Mitchell had told them that the eastbound stage wouldn't be leaving before eight-thirty, which gave them ample time to get some good hot food inside them before braving the penetrating chill outside.

Some little while later they returned to the lobby and settled their bill. Although Mitchell had assured them that the job would only take as long as it took to reach Little Cody and then ride back, there was no sense in keeping their room. If the snow should come in sufficient volume and they found themselves stranded in the mountains, their room here wasn't going to do them much good.

They went back upstairs and gathered their gear altogether. In addition to their saddlebags and long guns – Sam's .56 calibre Spencer carbine and Matt's longer and generally more accurate Winchester .44/40 – their belongings also included a fat tan and white Abyssinian cat with expressive sea-green eyes. This was Mitzi, who had slunk into Sam's life about four or five years earlier and been a permanent fixture ever since. He never had discovered where she'd originally come from, or why she had chosen to adopt him, but he had named her after a Cypriot he'd known down in Black Rock, Nevada, and the cat had accepted the name just as readily as she had accepted him.

From the hotel the Texans went down to Buckman's Livery with the cat padding along at their heels. The day was bitterly cold and they walked with gloved hands balled into fists and jackets buttoned to the chin. It looked as if Mitchell had been right to predict snow for today: the sky was heavy with ominous-looking, dishwater-grey clouds.

On the way, they stopped off quickly to buy some extra supplies for the journey. Further along the street, a big bottle-green Concord coach with enormous yellow wheels stood outside the Wells Fargo office, a glistening six-horse team standing hipshot and heads-down in the traces, expelling vapour into the milky sunshine. Beyond the town, the Bighorns rose in tall, seamed splendour, thickly forested and with the highest granite or sandstone scarps partially obscured by low, cottony clouds.

Sam and Matt entered the stable, paid their bill and readied their horses for the coming ride. Sam favoured a gnarled old strawberry roan named Charlie, Matt a smaller, nimble-footed cow-pony. Just before he swung up into the saddle, Sam scooped Mitzi up off the hay-strewn dirt floor and deposited her into his right-side saddlebag. The cat gave him a sleepy blink and a plaintive meow, then ducked out of sight beneath the flap.

Outside, a sudden commotion compromised mainly of yells and whip-cracks told them that the stage was pulling out, dead on time. As they led their horses out into the rutted street, they were just in time to see the coach rocking and swaying off out of town, following a rough, winding trail as it snaked up across a broad slope covered in wheatgrass and redtops, heading towards distant foothills and the first of many stands of timber, mostly cottonwood and willow at this low elevation.

Constable Mitchell was standing on the boardwalk outside the depot, watching the coach leave. He turned as Sam and Matt cantered up, and raised one gloved hand in salute. They returned it and slowed down for a brief word, content to allow the stage to pull out some distance ahead of them for two good reasons.

In the first place, they didn't want the guard glancing back and spotting them. If that happened, and he got the wrong idea about them, he might go and do something foolish. In the second place, if Mitchell was right, and someone *was* trying to intimidate the judge, Sam wanted the element of surprise if they should try anything more between here and their destination.

Sam produced a cigar and lit up. A cold wind shafted down off the higher country, making their mounts sidestep nervously as they sensed the coming storm. While they chatted, the stage-coach lumbered and lurched along the wheelmarked trail, bouncing over every dip and swell. Soon it vanished around a bend and was obscured from further sight by a stand of tormented-looking hawthorn trees.

That was their cue to move out. Saying their farewells, they set off at a steady lope as the sky to the north grew darker and darker.

They followed the trail upward, through heavy forests of aspen and spruce. They passed streams bursting with trout, then rode down through bowls of land rich with bluegrass and littered with buttercups. Every so often one or the other of them would gallop out ahead, just to make sure the coach was still moving along without problem.

The morning wore on. The Texans rode in silence. It was too cold for talk, even if they'd been so inclined. Sam, who felt the cold more keenly than his younger companion, had been hoping the day would warm up, but if anything the mercury dropped still further.

As they rode higher, sturdy pines took over from the flimsier timber, mostly lodgepole and ponderosa. The wind picked up even stronger, literally sweeping down from the dark north, and they swapped a look when the first flakes of snow began to feather down from clouds that boiled like dirty linen.

Ten minutes later the snow started falling harder, and with little option, Sam and Matt turned off the trail and into some sheltering trees. Visibility was cut dramatically as white patches began to spread across the land and then link up with others until at length there was nothing out there but a spreading mantle of snow.

Still, at least the timber kept the worst of it off, and provided some protection from the sharp, gusting wind. It was quiet beneath the eerie, olive-green canopy of trees, quiet and gloomy.

'We musta been crazy to put ourselves forward for this,' Sam muttered. He took out a fresh cigar, produced a match and struck it. Almost immediately the wind blew it out. He repeated the procedure twice more. On each occasion the wind snuffed out the flame. Eventually he gave up with a curse.

'Might's well make a fire and boil up some coffee,' Matt suggested, hiding a smile. 'That coach up ahead's sure not about to go much further in this weather.'

Sam nodded and stuffed the cigar back into his pocket.

It was then that they heard the gunshot.

It cracked out across the high country, leaving a dying echo in its wake, and snapped both men out of their cold-induced stupor. Calming the suddenly-skittish horses, they listened for any further sounds, but by this time even the echo had faded and all that was left was the soughing and moaning of the wind.

All thought of coffee now forgotten, they kicked the horses to speed and rode swiftly towards the sound of the shot, hoofbeats muffled by a thick carpet of fallen needles.

The trees stretched in a wide belt for maybe a quarter of a mile. The two men were engulfed by trunks stained green by moss and lichen. After a time the timber thinned, and when they came out the far side they found themselves back on the trail.

The snow wasn't falling quite so fast anymore, although the sky was still the colour of slate. Directly ahead of them, the trail led up over another steep hill. Here and there grey-green sage and greasebrush thrust up out of the white carpet. The churned marks left in the snow by the stage and the six-horse team were already filling in.

Sam swung down, leaving Charlie ground-hitched, and pulled his Spencer from its sheath. Then he ran in a crouch up through the snow to the brow of the hill, where he went down behind some of the screening brush to survey the country below.

On the far side of the hill the land opened out into a far-reaching valley. Evening star, forget-me-not, goldenrod, sourdock and flax poked doggedly up out of the thin snow-cover like splashes of paint on an artist's pallet. Away to the north and south, Douglas firs formed rough boundaries to the trail, spreading right down to the heart of the valley and then up to the far purple hills further northeast.

The stagecoach was stalled at the foot of the slope, about a hundred and fifty yards below. Two men with bandanas pulled up over their lower faces sat their horses in front of the vehicle with handguns drawn. The driver and shotgun guard were both sitting up on the high seat with their hands in the air.

Sam squinted. There was nothing to distinguish either of the masked men. Neither did the drifting snow do anything to help him get a closer look at them. They were just men on horse-back, no different from any others, save that they had guns in their hands and they looked just ornery enough to use them.

He heard a sound behind him. Glancing around he saw Matt coming up the grade to join him, Winchester held across his belly, face red with cold, breath misting the chilly noon.

He turned back to face the coach below, wondering if the masked men were would-be robbers or representatives of those people Mitchell had mentioned who would prefer the trial in Little Cody not to go ahead.

One of the road agents yanked on his horse's reins and the animal walked off to one side of the coach. The man said something. The Texans couldn't hear what it was, but they both saw the man's bandana puff in and out in time with the words.

There was a moment then when nothing happened. The man spoke again, his voice rising sharply, and this time Sam and Matt both heard what he said.

'You inside the coach! Get out, I say!'

A moment passed. The cold horses side-stepped restlessly. Another blast of wind made snowflakes spiral to earth in crazy patterns. Then the nearside door pushed open and the passengers, three of them, clambered down into the dying blizzard.

There was a woman, a bearded man of perhaps thirty-five, and the judge. The woman was dressed in a flowing maroon-coloured dress and matching over-jacket and hat. She stood out like a bloodstain against the chalky backdrop. Automatically she held out her reticule to the masked men, but the one who had ordered them out of the coach in the first place made a negative gesture with the Colt in his hand and then jabbed it at the judge.

That told them all they really needed to know.

'F-for God's sake, mister!' the stagecoach driver called down. 'If you're g-gonna rob us, jus' get on with it! We tarry here much longer an' we're not gonna be able to get this here coach movin' again!'

It was true. Already snow was starting to pile up against the wheels and bleach the sides of the shifting, steaming horses. Slowly but inexorably the valley was filling in with snow, and the snow was thickening up into drifts.

The masked man who had heeled his horse to the side of the trail inclined his head. All they could see of him were his green eyes, his raw, chapped cheekbones and a glimpse of red-fair hair poking out from beneath the brown hat he wore tied down with a scarf.

His horse shifted beneath him, making a soft, creaking noise as it compacted the snow beneath its hooves. At last the man said, 'All right. You two – get back inside the coach. No, not you, old man. You stay right where you are.'

Judge Moffat glared up at the man, his punished lips thinning down and his jaw muscles working. He was scared. Of course he was. But he was also getting old, and sometimes the older you got, the less there was to frighten you.

The bearded passenger standing beside him, like a grizzly bear in his thick overcoat, spoke up. 'Just what the devil–'

'Shut up and do like I say.'

But with a lady present, he felt impelled to stand fast. 'But we cannot just leave this man with you! Who *are* you, anyway? Just what is it you're planning to do–'

Without warning, the masked man jabbed his Colt skyward and fired another shot. The handgun jumped in his fist, blasting flame and lead into the overcast, where the wind whipped its thunder away. The woman cried out and reached up to cover her ears. Taken by surprise, the bearded man cringed.

'Get inside, I said!'

The bearded man turned and looked at the judge. He looked frustrated by his impotence. The judge nodded to him, almost frighteningly calm by comparison, and indicated that he should do as they had told him.

Clearly reluctant to leave him at the questionable mercy of these men, the bearded passenger nevertheless turned away and helped the tearful woman up into the coach, glancing back at their tormentors all the while. The coach creaked on its leather thoroughbraces as they climbed aboard, Judge Moffat watching them through expressionless brown eyes as snow beaded on the lenses of his spectacles and gathered on his shoulders and the brim of his hat.

The door closed and the masked men joined each other at the side of the trail. 'On your way,' growled their spokesman.

The driver looked down at him imploringly, equally loath to abandon such a venerable old gentleman as the judge out here in the middle of nowhere.

But the green eyes showing above the bandana were as cold and unfeeling as the weather itself. 'On your way, I said,' the spokesman repeated, cocking his Colt again for emphasis.

The Jehu looked hurriedly away from him, ashamed by his lack of courage and anxious to avoid further trouble, then gathered the reins around his knobbly fists. Kicking off the brake, he slapped the nearest team-horses across the rump and the stagecoach abruptly lurched into motion, slowly rolling away from the judge and his captors, leaving them isolated there, completely enveloped by the immensity of the valley.

That made things a little less tricky.

Up to then, Constable Mitchell's two deputies had been caught between the devil and hell, unwilling to throw down on the masked men for fear of putting the exposed passengers and crew at risk. But now, as the stagecoach shushed and slewed away through the snow, the risk was reduced, albeit only slightly.

There was still the safety of the judge to consider.

Although Sam and Matt were pretty fair shots, neither of them could guarantee to hit their respective targets first time around, not in this weather. And in the time it would take them to try again, the masked men could easily put a bullet into the judge and light out.

Before they did anything else, then, they'd

have to draw the attention of the judge's assailants away from him in some way, and hope to God that the judge himself would get out of the line of fire fast, once all hell broke loose.

Sam turned to Matt. He had a plan, of sorts. As they slipped and skidded back down the slope toward their horses, Sam outlined it briefly. It wasn't much, but right then there wasn't time for anything more fancy.

At the foot of the hill they thrust their long guns away and vaulted up into their saddles. They had some riding to do before the shooting started.

Leaning heavily on his cane, Judge Moffat watched the stagecoach shrink until it looked more like a pea in the distance. The smaller it got, the more acute became his sense of exile. The solitude of the valley was further intensified by the peculiar silence that had engulfed the high country, the odd, total silence that always accompanies heavy snow.

At last he turned his attention back to the masked men. The one who had so far done all the talking, the previous evening as well as today, said, 'You know, you must have a lousy sense o' direction, judge. We told you to forget all about goin' on to Little Cody. We told you to get back where you came from. An' yet here you are.' He leaned forward, saddle creaking. 'What is it with you? You deaf, stupid or jus' plain stubborn?'

Judge Moffat drew himself up to his full if modest height. His mouth was dry but somehow he managed to speak without his voice cracking. 'Who *are* you men?' he asked, peering up at them.

'We're the men who don't care to see you up in Little Cody,' said the spokesman. 'We're the men who told you that we'd kill you if you kept a-comin'.'

The judge sucked in his breath. 'And … and is that … what you propose to do?'

'You had your choice,' said the second man, breaking his silence at last.

'Am I at least entitled to know … *why* I

have to die?'

'Aw now, you ain't that stupid. You know why, or leastways you must have a pretty fair notion.'

The judge *did* have a notion, of course. It wasn't exactly difficult to figure out. But he was trying to delay the inevitable in the vain hope that these men would suddenly see just how momentous – and irreversible – the act they were planning really was, and per- haps show clemency instead.

'The trial?' he hazarded.

The spokesman inclined one shoulder. 'I ain't sayin' yes, an' I ain't sayin' no.'

He flipped open the Colt's loading gate and turned the cylinder to empty out the spent shell-cases, then set about replacing them with fresh loads.

The judge had noticed that both men shared the same colouring, but that the spokesman's hair was somewhat shorter than that of his companion, who wore it to well below collar length. He concluded that they must be related, probably brothers. But where Long Hair's voice was high and nervous, the other man's was deeper and more controlled, the voice of a man who didn't give a damn.

At last the spokesman finished reloading and snapped the gate shut with a sudden, metallic crack.

After another moment he said, 'All right, old man. Turn around an' start walkin'.'

Lew Moffat frowned. '*What* was that?'

'You heard me. You're turnin' around an' goin' back the way you came, judge. Only you're gonna do it the hard way. You're gonna *walk* it. Every rod of it. An' next time we tell you to do a thing, you'll *do* it, 'cause you won't dare do anythin' else.'

Beneath his cuts and bruises, the judge blanched. 'Now see here! You … you can't be serious! I … I could never walk all that–'

The masked man pointed his handgun in the judge's direction and fired another shot. The judge flinched and stumbled backwards as the bullet tore into the ground at his feet and sent up a great geyser of snow.

Beneath his bandana, the masked man's voice became a snarl. 'Oh, we're serious all right, you old bastard, an' you better believe it! *Now get movin'!*'

The judge's mouth clamped tight. Grown used to the respect his position gave him, he was furious at the treatment he was receiving now. But there was no sense in antagonising these men any further. They could easily shoot him and be done with it. At least this way he had a chance to stay alive, albeit an admittedly slim one.

In defeat he started to turn around, but just as he did so he caught a movement from the edge of his vision. A rider suddenly burst from the timber about ninety or a hundred yards to the south, a strange, ululating cry carrying out ahead of him and a sixgun winking flame and thunder across the valley towards his captors.

Instinctively the masked men hipped around that way, taken totally by surprise.

'What–?'

In the very next moment, a second rider

broke from the timber fringing the north side of the trail forty yards away, also yelling at the top of his lungs to increase the confusion of the masked men, and firing a handgun wildly into the air.

'Jesus Christ!'

Unnerved by all the noise, the mounts of the masked men began to prance and caper. Yanking their reins tight, knowing that whoever these newcomers were, they weren't friendly, the judge's assailants turned their guns toward them and set about returning fire.

Suddenly the valley came alive with the echo and crackle of gunfire. As confused as the masked men, but realising dimly that these howling in-comers were offering him a chance to escape the clutches of his would-be killers, the judge laboured over to the edge of the trail, flung himself down onto his stomach and folded his arms over his head.

Meanwhile, Long Hair's horse reared up on its hind legs and the man himself slid out of the saddle, described a loose, awkward back-flip and bounced against the snow.

Squirming on the ground, cold seeping through his greatcoat, the judge chanced to look up. The spokesman, as he had come to think of the man, was twisting this way and that around his horse's tossing head, alternately firing his handgun at the man on the zig-zagging strawberry roan, then at his companion on the charging pony, making them keep their distance. The judge felt certain that his eardrums would burst, the nose was so great.

Scant yards from him, the spokesman yelled at Long Hair, telling him to get back up and give him a hand. Snow exploded beneath the horses' hooves as they stamped and darted this way and that, the spokesman's voice reverberating across the valley.

Long Hair had scrambled up almost as soon as he fell down, and now, scooping up his fallen Colt, he started after his side-stepping horse. But caught up in the heady excitement of the situation, not stopping to think about the consequences, the judge decided on impulse to take a hand in the proceedings himself.

Shoving up onto his feet, he waded after Long Hair and cried out, *'Stay right where you are...!'*

Right where you are ... right where you are...!

Hearing him, Long Hair spun around to face him and brought his Colt up fast.

The judge struck out with his cane, bringing the sturdy stick down across the other man's wrist. Long Hair yelped and dropped the weapon at once, and the judge, pressing his advantage, brought the cane around in a wide sweep that caught him alongside the head.

Long Hair screamed, brought both hands up to his left ear and staggered sideways under the impact of the blow. His voice was pure panic as he bawled, *'Aw Christ, you broke my jaw!'*

Broke my jaw ... broke my jaw...!

Up in the saddle, the spokesman twisted around, saw what the judge had done and, with a string of curses, pointed his Colt right at the old man and pulled the trigger.

The Colt went *click*.

Empty!

In that same moment a searing pain punched him in the left shoulder and from the corner of his eye he saw a mixture of blood and meat spray out through the sleeve of his sheepskin jacket.

Two seconds passed before he realised he'd been hit, and then his scream came out more like a howl than anything else, the howl soon turning to a roar of rage and defiance.

'*Damn you!*'

Damn you … damn you…!

But even through all the pain and anger he knew there was no time to get even now. Like it or not, their only recourse was flight.

He yelled for his companion to catch his horse and ride, then rammed his heels into his own mount's flanks and tore off through the snow, holding the animal to a weird, see-sawing gallop, swaying in the saddle as he sent the horse down the trail after the stage-coach.

He rode madly for about three hundred yards, then veered to the left and cut across country, heading for the screening trees. His partner, still holding his throbbing face, snatched up his mount's trailing reins, threw himself up across his hull and followed right behind him.

Within moments the pair of them were out of sight, swallowed up by the timber.

The wind picked up and the snow started to fall harder again as the Texans converged on the judge.

For a while the men and horses just stood there, blowing clouds into the air as they got their breath back. Then Sam said, 'You all right, judge?' and the judge, recognising them at last, said in surprise, 'Mr Judge? Mr Dury? Whatever–'

Sam cut in, 'You got George Mitchell to thank, judge. He had an idea somethin' like this might happen.'

The sounds of battle had made the driver stall the coach partway across the valley floor. Now Matt rode out a-ways, took out his Winchester and fired three shots into the air. A moment later the shotgun guard fired three shots in response.

Sam, meanwhile, had produced a cigar, turned away from the wind and, hunching his shoulders, was attempting to light it. Without looking around, he said, 'Constable Mitchell figures there might be some folks don't want you to reach Little Cody an' try a man for murder. He thinks it was them who took a crack at you las' night.'

As Matt rode back in and stepped down to kneel and examine the spreading crimson stain where one of them had hit the spokesman in the arm, he said, 'That about the size of it, judge?'

Taking a deep breath, Judge Moffat admitted, 'Yes, gentlemen. I fear I *am* being intimidated.'

'Got any idea who they are, them fellers?'

'Not at this stage. But I don't suppose it

will be difficult to find out, once I reach Little Cody.' Spreading his hands, he said, 'Gentlemen ... how can I ever thank you for your help?'

'Forget it,' growled Sam, giving up on trying to light the smoke. Instead he scanned the broad sweep of the valley, as much of it as he could see through the swirling white. 'I don't suppose they'll try anythin' more now. We plugged one of 'em, an' it looks like you gave the other one a heckuva headache. But you never know. We'll ride escort on you the rest of the way in, jus' to make sure.'

'But gentlemen,' Moffat protested. 'I am in your debt, make no mistake about it. But I cannot expect you to keep on risking your lives on my account.'

A rare twitch of a smile touched Sam's narrow mouth as he shoved the cigar back into his pocket and set about reloading his Remington. 'Well then, let's get one thing straight right at the outset, Your Honour. That's the second time in as many days that them fellers've thrown lead at me'n Matt.

That makes it kinda personal.'

'Sam's right, judge,' Matt said, indicating that Moffat should mount his horse so that he could lead the animal down to the waiting coach. 'Much more of their shenanigans and we're apt to turn mean. *Real* mean. And *then* those fellers better watch out.'

THREE

With the judge safely back inside the coach and a brief mixture of introduction and explanation offered to the passengers and crew, they ploughed on through the renewed storm, squinting against the driving snow, the horses moving reluctantly, and at a stumble-footed crawl.

They headed deeper and higher into the Bighorns, the wind shrieking and the snow churning around them. The afternoon grew as dull as early evening. At times they lost the trail and came to a dead stop, and the driver had to use every trick in the book to induce his spooky, worn-down team-animals to back up or go around, and then move on.

One hour passed more like three. Men and animals were chilled to the marrow. But eventually they saw lights up ahead and as they drew nearer, so the welcome buildings of a log-built, snow-covered roadhouse came into sight a couple-hundred yards ahead and below them.

The driver braked and the coach groaned to a halt, dusted white along the sides and wheels, thick with snow across the baggage-laden roof. Sam, riding beside him, reined in and glanced stiff-necked up at him. 'You all right up there, driver?'

The driver had been muttering something to the guard. Now he turned back to Sam and nodded. His face was partially hidden behind a tugged-up scarf, but his eyes were visible and they looked uneasy. 'Uh-huh.'

'Come on then, let's get a move on. That there roadhouse is about the most invitin'-lookin' thing I seen all day!'

But now the driver's voice matched the look in his eyes. 'If it's all the same to you, I think we'll press on without stoppin'.'

'*What?* Are you joshin' me? Your horses're spent, mister, an' so're we.'

'I'd as soon keep us movin',' the driver

insisted. 'We're way behind schedule as it is. 'Sides, we linger here an' this snow keeps fallin', we'll find ourselves stranded. Best to keep on the move till we reach Little Cody.'

Sam fisted the reins over his saddlehorn. Even bundled up as he was, he was aching with the cold. He couldn't even imagine what it must be like for the passengers, huddled up inside the unglazed coach. He glanced out ahead once more, to the inviting amber lights showing at the distant road-house windows. He could almost feel the wave of warm air that would greet them as soon as they shoved in through the heavy front door and headed for the stove. Pots filled with scalding coffee, black and sweet, just how he liked it, and a couple bowls of good hot tater stew would set them up for the final leg of the run.

He couldn't understand the driver's reluctance to stop here. 'Fact, there was something about it that struck him as downright odd. Matt must have thought so too, because he asked from the other side of the box, 'There something you're not telling us about this place, mister?'

The driver dropped his eyes to his lap. Next to him, the guard said impatiently, 'Look, we just want to get to Little Cody, make out our report to the agent and then get home to our wives an' kids.'

The driver looked up and held Sam's eyes again, angry and defiant now. Clearly he wasn't going to stop at the roadhouse for anyone. Sam glared at him, wondering why. But in the next moment he relaxed. There didn't have to be any other reason than the ones he and the guard had already given him. It came to him that this had been a long and taxing day, and maybe he was starting to jump at shadows.

'What's the delay here?' the bearded passenger asked, poking his head out the window.

Sam glanced back at him. 'No delay, friend,' he replied. Looking back at the driver he said, 'We're movin' out again right now.'

The driver slapped the reins and the coach

moved on, snow squirming out from under the spinning iron tyres, the coach itself rocking as another icy blast caught it sideways on.

They crawled down the trail and on past the roadhouse. No-one came to the windows or door to see who they were, although the sounds of their passing must have carried to the occupants of the place. Sam glanced sideways at the lamplit, frosty windows, still thinking about the warmth and comfort that was so near and yet so far.

Then the roadhouse was behind them and they were forging ahead again, higher and deeper, swallowed by granite canyons etched with unimaginably ancient and indecipherable Indian writings.

There was something hypnotic about the relentless push forward, the jogging of their straining horses, the amount of concentration required just to keep going and not spill from the saddle. With no chance of further trouble from the judge's enemies, at least for the time being, Sam allowed his mind to wander. He longed for a cigar, but knew it would be impossible to enjoy in such inhospitable conditions, even supposing he could get the blessed thing alight, which was doubtful.

Then, quite suddenly, the wind dropped and the snow slowed from a torrent to a trickle, and at last he could chance a look up and over their surroundings without the wind stripping the skin off his face and stealing the breath out of his lungs.

They were crossing flats between one belt of whitened timber and another, with more forested hills shelving skyward beyond it. A tributary of the Tongue wound in a series of sweeping S's across the pristine plain, already sluggish and lumpy with forming ice. They picked up speed on the flats, though not by much, then entered the far timber. Here the bearded passenger shoved his head out through the window again and asked if it might be possible to stop for a while and boil up some coffee, because in his opinion both the lady and the judge were showing signs of hypothermia.

Sam had never heard of hypothermia, but he got the general idea and called up to the driver, 'How about it?'

This time he received no argument. The driver hauled back on the reins and stepped on the brake, and the trail-worn coach came to a springy halt among the trees. 'You got fifteen minutes,' the man said, climbing down to inspect the exhausted team-animals.

As the passengers disembarked gratefully, Matt fixed a small fire, filled their old enamel coffee pot with water and beans and then set it at the fire's edge to heat through. The passengers and crew came to stand around the flames and hold their hands out. There was no real conversation, just a few cold and weary noises. Sam took Mitzi out of her saddlebag and set her down so that she could stretch her legs. The cat looked grateful for the opportunity to pad away and explore their new surroundings.

The coffee went quite a way towards perking them all up, and twenty minutes later, with cramped muscles exercised, bladders discreetly emptied and the coffee warming them all from the inside out, they were ready to move on.

The afternoon darkened still further, but the snow held off. By the time the lights of Little Cody came into sight an hour later, night was approaching fast from the east.

It was around six o'clock when the driver finally tooled the coach down Little Cody's slushy, torchlit main street, and because they were about four or five hours behind time, their arrival attracted considerable interest from those locals still out and about to witness it.

The town itself was something of a jumble, with log-built stores, restaurants and other places of commerce crowding up to each other in a string of crazy mis-matches that ran the length of the gently-sloping, stony thoroughfare. Bigger residential houses and cabins lifted away across the spruce-dotted slopes to the north and south. There were no boardwalks here, save for those odd stretches of planking that some of the storekeepers had thought to lay out in front of their establishments.

As Sam and Matt fell back to ride behind the coach, they saw that Little Cody was every inch a mining town. Even though it was the supper hour, even though most everything had been covered up and slowed down by the recent blizzard, the place was still buzzing. The street was choked by wagon-traffic. Men puffed up to twice their normal size by thick, sensible racoon-skin coats were scurrying here or there on one important errand or another. Flaming torches cast twitching shadows over snow-capped piles of trimmed lumber and stacked barrels.

The coach drew up outside the small Wells Fargo office. The agent was waiting for them out front, fidgeting with his Ingersoll watch. There followed the usual bustle of men unloading the baggage from the roof and local folks meeting the new arrivals with hugs or handshakes.

Sam and Matt pulled their horses over to one side of it all, waiting for Judge Moffat to make an appearance. When he did, he looked slightly the worse for wear, but offered them a cheery enough wave as he shuffled over.

Clearing his throat, he said, 'Well, I made it – thanks to you.'

'You got a place to stay, judge?' asked Sam.

'I believe that has already been arranged for me, yes.'

Sam touched his hat-brim. 'Well, we better go see what we can rustle up for ourselves, then.'

'Very good, gentlemen. Oh, and one other thing.'

'What's that?'

'Please be kind enough to instruct whichever hotel you choose that I will be picking up your tab,' Moffat replied. When they made to object, the judge raised one hand to silence them. 'Really, gentlemen. I insist.'

'Well,' Sam replied, low-voiced. 'We'll see.'

They turned their horses away from the

depot and walked them further along the street, searching for a stable and a hotel. As it turned out they found the two in one when they reined in before a large frame building, at two storeys probably the tallest in Little Cody, which had the simple legend HOTEL painted in fancy script above the door.

Within a quarter of an hour the horses were contentedly munching grain in the stable behind the hotel, and the Texans themselves were back out on the frozen street, having deposited Mitzi and their gear in an austere but passable room over-looking the main drag.

Their priority now was to get something good and filling to eat. And Little Cody, a twenty-four-hour-a-day-town if Sam had ever seen one, looked just the kind of place to supply it. Around them, Main was still a riot of activity. Tinkling pianos and lilting, female voices drifted out of the many saloons they passed. Once they glanced in through the oiled deerhide windows of one establishment and found it packed to the rafters with mostly miner-types, big, bearded men in from the iron ore and copper mines higher in the surrounding hills.

At length they found a restaurant and went inside. The warm, fragrant air was a balm to their windburnt faces. The place was crowded, and noisy with chatter. Steam fogged the windows with misty droplets. Finding space at one of the trestle tables, they shouldered in among still more miners, sat down and ordered the special, which was rabbit pie and mashed potatoes.

In a town where people came and went every hour of the day, they were pleased to see that they attracted no special attention. In any case, it looked as if their fellow diners had other matters to occupy them – specifically the trial over which Judge Moffat was here to preside.

'They should just hang the bastard an' be done with it,' opined one man a few feet further along from them, spitting food across the table as he spoke. 'Why go through all the rigmarole of a trial? We all *know* he did it!' The man sat back, fisted his coffee mug and concluded, 'They should string him up now, tonight, that's what I say. Hang him and let him rot there as a lesson to the rest of his heathen kind!'

Sam and Matt glanced at each other across the table. As strangers here, they didn't really have a clue what this business was all about, and were tempted to ask someone, but with local feeling so strong, that might not be the wisest idea.

'That's all well and good,' another man called down from the far end of the table, his knife and fork almost lost in his enormous, work-scarred hands. 'But these things gotta be done accordin' to the law, Braden. You *know* that.'

'Fred's right,' said a third man. 'We start takin' the law into our own hands, where does it all end? That's why these things hafta be done the proper way. So we all know where we stand.'

The big man who was all for hanging,

Braden, grunted something and shovelled some more food into his mouth. He had a flushed, sweaty look that told them he'd been drinking, and that the alcohol was turning him belligerent. 'You're missin' the point,' he replied. 'All right. So the devil stands trial. The judge finds him guilty. They give him a length o' rope to dangle from. So where's the sense of draggin' it out? A few decent men take him out and do the job tonight, they're only carryin' out what the law'll decree tomorrow or the next day.'

The conversation went back and forth across the table. Whatever had happened here had obviously outraged the locals. But opinion was divided over what should be done with the accused man, although the majority favoured a quick drop and a slow death.

It wasn't exactly the kind of conversation that was designed to aid a man's digestion, but by this time Sam and Matt were so hungry, and the food so good, that nothing could put them off for long. Fortunately, the place quietened down once Braden and his followers finished eating and headed for the nearest saloon, leaving the Texans to top off their meal with apple pie and coffee.

Having finally ironed the pleats out of their stomachs, they settled their bill, pulled on their gloves, buttoned their jackets and stepped back out into the street, studying the sky with a range man's eye to the weather.

The clouds were looking ominous again, obscuring the moon and stars and promising yet more snow for the morrow.

Sam shook his head in despair. This was the one thing they'd been hoping to avoid – getting snowed-in up here. The journey down out of the mountains was already going to be difficult enough as it was. One more heavy snowfall and they'd be stuck here till spring thaw.

The saloons looked inviting, with their mixture of whiskey, women and rough, home-grown entertainment, but the Texans felt too tired to enjoy such undoubted attractions to the full, and decided to head back to the hotel instead. No sooner did Matt unlock the door than Mitzi brushed past them and scurried out into the hallway, headed for the stairs.

They turned to watch her go. Unlike them, she had slept the whole day through, apart from that one little episode when they'd had to do some hard riding and then tangle with the masked men. Now she was ready to explore the town.

'You behave yourself now, y'hear?' Sam called sternly to the cat's retreating back. 'I don't want you disgracin' yourself.'

She never even deigned to glance backwards.

They entered the dark room, took off their hats and unbuttoned their jackets. It was a relief to get in out of the wind. Again Sam thought about the word Constable Mitchell had used on them the previous evening. *Regulators.* He wasn't sure just how they'd fallen into such a trade. By accident? Maybe. As Mitchell had said, Sam was a peacemaker from way back. After all these years, he guessed it was in his blood to uphold the law. But Matt…

He watched Matt cross the room, lift the funnel on the lantern hanging from the centre of the ceiling and light the wick. As a dull, smoky glow pervaded the room, Sam frowned.

After Matt's ma had died, he'd gotten himself a job nursing cows close to the family home in Brownwood, Texas. But as the months rolled by, so he'd fallen in with the wrong crowd. Eventually they'd wandered up into the Sangre de Christos country of Colorado and decided to rob a small-town bank nearby. Trouble was, the bank was in a town where Sam packed a badge.

Sam set his weight down on the edge of one sagging mattress and took out the cigar he'd tried to smoke earlier. He hated to think what would have happened if Matt had gone ahead with the robbery. They hadn't seen each other for fifteen years or more, but there was still a bond between them. Bob

Dury, Matt's pa, had been the closest friend Sam had ever had, and Matt himself had always looked upon Sam as a kind of unofficial uncle.

But duty was duty. Sam would have tracked him down for sure. And then...?

Luckily, that situation never came to pass. Matt's so-called partners had turned on him when he tried to talk them out of the robbery, and leaving him badly beaten, had gone ahead with it anyway.

They'd left two people dead in their wake.

Sam had tracked them down and eventually they'd stood trial and were hanged. Matt had sided him towards the finish of the job, and one way or another they'd been siding each other ever since. And that was good. Because although Matt didn't know it, it was Sam, not Bob Dury, who was his natural father.

Sam clamped the cigar between his lips and fished out a phosphor. That one single afternoon of infidelity still troubled him, and he didn't like to think about it too much. He struck the match and was just about to touch it to the tip of the stogie when Matt, standing over by the window now, suddenly said, 'Better come and take a look at this, Sam. Looks like trouble brewing.'

Sam shook the match out and tossed it into the old sardine can on the bedside cabinet that was supposed to double for an ashtray. One of these days he was going to smoke that cigar, he told himself. But from the sound of Matt's voice, there were other matters demanding his attention right now, more important ones.

With the cigar still fixed in his mouth, he got up and went over to join his partner. He wiped a clear circle in the icy window and looked out. A knot of men had gathered in the streets beneath them, maybe fifty or sixty strong. Some of them were holding torches high overhead to light their passage down toward the marshal's office three-quarters of the way along the other side of the street.

Sam muttered the obvious. 'Lynch-mob.'

Matt nodded. 'It sure doesn't look like much of a liberty campaign.'

It sure didn't. They watched the mob tramp further down the street in a muddy brown tide. Through the glass they could hear a low, sinister babble rising up from them as they surged past. Then the man at their head turned to wave them further on, and Sam recognised the big, food-spitting man from the restaurant whose name was Braden.

He unplugged the cigar and stuffed it back into his pocket. He might've known a feller like that would cause trouble sooner or later. He'd seen this kind of situation too many times before. Take a rabble-rouser, a saloon, a drink, two drinks, several drinks. Before you knew it, the crowd had turned into a mob, an angry mob, and they would be out for blood. It didn't necessarily matter whose.

Braden's supporters were well and truly behind him, and the man himself strode on ahead like a five-star general. Handguns and rifles shone in the torchlight as they gathered in a half-circle around the marshal's office, having been joined by yet more people on the march down.

Braden grabbed a torch from the nearest man and held it high. He knew all the tricks, that one, knew exactly how to take charge and present a striking figure. 'Colbert!' he yelled. 'Colbert, there's a delegation here that wants a word with you!'

An expectant silence descended over the mob. As one, all eyes were focused on the thick, sturdy door of the squat, shuttered, log-built office and jailhouse.

Nothing happened for a moment. The whole of Little Cody stayed hushed. Then there came the sound of a bolt scraping back, and after that the door opened and the town marshal came out into the Arctic evening.

The Texans strained to get a better look at him. The first thing that struck them about him was his age – he didn't look like much more than a boy. He was of average height and muscular build, formally dressed in a shirt and string tie, his black jacket bulked out by a thick beige sweater. He wore his gunbelt high and twisted around so that the pocket rested on his left hipbone, the grips of his butt-forward, short-barrelled .38 within easy reach of his right hand.

Sam guessed he was about twenty one or two. Too damn' young for this kind of job. But as he faced the crowd, hands defiantly on hips, there was no fear or uncertainty in him, at least none that Sam could see, and he had to admire the boy for that.

The marshal, Colbert, had a squarish face, clean-shaven, with honest blue eyes, a short, snubbed nose and a wide mouth. 'It's Braden, isn't it?' he said at last. 'Al Braden?'

'Ayuh, it's Braden,' the miner replied with a nod. 'We've come for Tom Powell. We've tried him for his crimes an' found him guilty, an' now we're here to carry out the sentence for the court!'

'You mean you aim to hang him,' Colbert

said grimly.

'That's *exactly* what we mean,' Braden replied, and there was a muttering of approval from the men immediately behind him.

Marshal Colbert ranged his eyes across the gathering, trying to gauge just how many of these men were serious about what they were proposing, and how many would change their minds at the first sign of resistance. It was dispiriting to him to find that no man there tried to avoid his gaze, or showed any other sign of cracking.

'Well,' he said at length. 'I hate to disappoint you men, but there'll be no lynching here tonight or any other night. Judge Moffat just got into town earlier this evening. That means Tom Powell will stand trial tomorrow. Once all the evidence is in, it'll be up to the jury to decide whether or not he's guilty, and once they've decided that, it'll be up to the judge whether or not he hangs. You men won't have anything to do with it. You're not even residents of Little

Cody, most of you. Now turn around and get out of here. You're blocking the street with this assembly.'

Up at the hotel room window, Sam nodded his approval. It was as pretty a speech as he had ever heard, and not once had Colbert's voice betrayed any hint of uncertainty. With any sober crowd it might have turned the trick. But he'd already established that this wasn't a sober crowd. And if Sam was any judge of character – which he was – Braden wouldn't let a youngster fifteen years his junior get the better of him.

He was right.

'Stand aside, Colbert!' Braden grated, injecting more iron into his tone. 'It's common knowledge that Tom Powell murdered that little gal, just like he murdered all them others. Well, we've had enough of watchin' our women go in fear. We're gonna show him just how we treat killers in this town!'

A cheer rose up from the hardcore Braden supporters, and that communicated itself to the rest of them. These men weren't about to be turned away now. They were liquored-up, fired-up, and the prospect of watching a hanging offered them the kind of excitement few of them would ever otherwise know.

Braden took a pace forward. 'Step aside, Colbert,' he growled. 'We're comin' in.'

Colbert backed up a step and yanked out his .38. 'Stay right where you are, all of you, or so help me, I'll shoot the first man who tries to take Powell out of his cell!'

'And I'll shoot the second,' said a woman, coming out of the office to stand beside the marshal, a Henry repeater athwart her impressive chest.

A woman was the last person any of them expected to find taking a hand in the proceedings. She was quite tall, dressed in a white blouse and a long brown skirt. She wore a shawl around her shoulders against the bite of the evening, and as she planted herself there beside the marshal, there was no doubt in Sam's mind that she meant what she'd said, that she meant it and then some.

She was in her middle to late forties, with a fine oval face that was home to evenly-spaced china-blue eyes, a small, straight nose and soft, generous lips, now thinned down into a disapproving line as she surveyed the troublemakers. Her hair was thick and had once been the bright, summery colour of wheat, but now the years were bleaching it to a lighter, paler shade of yellow that was still becoming. She wore it gathered into a bun at the back of her head, with a few curly strands corkscrewing down in front of her small ears to frame a fashionably pale face.

The appearance of the woman worked two effects upon the situation. It startled the crowd and maybe put a few doubts into the minds of the men who had previously considered this to be such a good idea. But it also gave the young marshal something new to worry about, and sensing his sudden distraction, Braden quickly seized the upper hand.

'Aw, now, Mrs Colbert,' he said. 'Stand aside, if you will, ma'am. We don't want to tangle with no woman. It's to make Little Cody a safer place for you women that we're here! But we mean to hang that murderin' devil tonight, have no doubt about it!'

He came forward and the rest of the crowd followed him in a surge. They closed to within another four feet of the jailhouse before the woman, Mrs Colbert, brought the Henry around on them.

'Not another step, Mr Braden!' she snapped, desperation edging her tone. 'Before God, I swear it!'

Trying to keep his eye on the mob, the marshal said, 'Ma...'

But by this time, Braden was near enough to reach out and grab the repeater, which is exactly what he did, moving so fast that Mrs Colbert was caught completely by surprise as he yanked the weapon away from her.

Matt had seen enough. Turning away from the window he said, 'Sam...?'

But Sam was already way ahead of him, over on the other side of the room, his Spencer in one fist, tossing Matt's Winchester to him with the other.

'Let's go,' he said tightly.

Down in the street, Braden seized the advantage and twisted the long gun around so that it was pointed at the marshal.

'Zack!' he called without turning his head. 'Take his gun!'

A tall, skinny man in a heavy twill jacket came forward and tore Colbert's .38 from his hand. Colbert's face was livid. Going over to stand beside his mother, he said breathlessly, 'I mean this, Braden! You take Tom Powell out of here tonight and so help me, *you'll* be the one standing trial for murder in the morning!'

Braden was unmoved. 'That's where you're wrong, marshal. In the mornin' these good people will *thank* me for what I did here tonight!'

He reached out one thick arm, shoved the younger man aside and made to stride forward through the door and into the office. It was in that instant that a rifle-shot suddenly shattered the night and the bullet itself sizzled over the heads of the forward-moving crowd, stopping them in their tracks.

Braden spun around as the others backed up behind him, a curse on his lips. He narrowed his eyes, trying to see who had dared to come to the defence of the man they were going to hang. But no-one was there. The upper half of the street was empty ... wasn't it?

Suddenly Braden's skin started crawling as he heard the steady, regular thud of men walking slowly down toward them. Then he caught a movement in the darkness and straightened out of the crouch into which he had instinctively fallen. Two men strode into a pool of orange light thirty feet away, long guns held across their chests, cold-reddened faces immobile, seemingly carved from granite.

The newcomers were the centre of attention as they came unhurriedly up onto the planking that fronted the marshal's office, halted beside the marshal and Mrs Colbert and then turned to face the crowd.

The wind picked up and tugged at the flames licking and dancing atop the scattered torches. It was cold enough to freeze a man's tongue to his teeth, but incredibly Marshal Colbert was sweating. He said, 'Who—'

Sam cut him off. 'Later, boy.'

He said it without taking his eyes off the mob. The mood they were in, he couldn't afford to. But though the odds were lousy – about twenty to one by his reckoning, if you included the woman – this business hinged on the actions of just one man. Braden.

He settled his mild grey eyes on the man. Braden was in his late thirties, about three inches taller than Sam and seventy pounds heavier. He had a jowly, surprisingly pale face beneath his thick, matted black beard, and his eyes were almost lost in the squeeze of flesh between his heavy brow and his bloated cheeks.

Sam held his appraising stare for so long that when he finally moved, the bigger man flinched. But Sam only passed his Spencer back and to the side, offering it to Mrs Colbert.

'If you would, ma'am?' he asked politely.

As surprised as the rest of them, the woman took the carbine before she properly knew what she was doing.

Addressing Braden, keeping his voice low and friendly, Sam said, 'I heard you shootin' your mouth off down at that cafe earlier on, Braden. You sure talk up a powerful argument. Strikes me you should'a gone into politics.'

Braden frowned, unable to get a handle on him. 'An' who're you?' he asked at last, warily.

Sam didn't answer immediately. His eyes dropped to the Henry repeater the other man had snatched away from Mrs Colbert. He reached forward slowly and casually, so's not to spook the big miner into doing anything rash, and though Braden resisted at first, he gently tugged the rifle towards him until the barrel was pressed dead-centre against his chest.

Then his eyes went cold.

'I'll tell you who I am,' he said. 'I'm the only thing standin' betwixt you an' the feller you're so all-fired anxious to string up, that's who I am. You understand me, Braden? If you want to get to him, all you got to do is pull that itty-bitty trigger there an' blow me to hell. That's all. After that, you can walk right in an' help yourself. No-one'll stop you. No-one'd dare. My word on it.'

Marshal Colbert said, 'Hey, now...'

To one side of him, Matt hissed softly, 'Shut up.'

And out front of them all, Sam said quietly, 'Well, Braden? How about it?'

FOUR

Braden looked at him as if he'd just grown an extra set of ears. Around them, the other men edged forward to see what he would do. The wind whipped at hat-brims and coat-flaps. Somewhere out in the darkness a coyote howled.

'You're crazy,' Braden breathed at last, and made to lower the Henry, but Sam grabbed at the barrel and kept it right where it was, shoved hard into his chest.

'What is it, Braden?' he asked with a frown. 'You never killed a man before?' He slapped himself in the chest, so suddenly that Braden flinched again. 'Hell, what're you waitin' for? I'm givin' you the chance to kill two in one evenin'!'

In the background, the skinny man called Zack muttered darkly, 'Call his bluff, Al.

Time's a-wastin'.'

Knowing that he had to do something, Braden said righteously, 'Executin' a man's not the same as killin' him.'

Sam shook his head. 'Don't bet on it. It all comes down to the same thing, Braden. Snuffin' out a life. Now, if a judge says this here Powell hangs 'cause of what he's supposed to've done to this girl – he hangs. That's justice. If you kill a man 'cause he's tryin' to kill *you,* that's self-defence. But you go ahead an' do what you're fixin' to do here tonight, an' that's killin', pure an' simple. Don't go dressin' it up jus' to make it easier to swallow.'

Getting edgy now, shifting his weight from one foot to the other, Braden said through clenched teeth, 'You're strainin' my patience awful hard, mister.'

Sam's grin was tight and cool. 'Well, I'm right sorry 'bout that,' he replied mockingly. 'But tell me somethin'. Why is it that I'm givin' you a chance to get at this here Powell, an' yet you're not takin' it? Why is it that I'm strainin' your patience so bad but you're not doin' anythin' about it? Why *is* that, Braden?'

'Punch his ticket, Al, an' let's get on with it,' Zack grumbled in a low voice.

'You want me to tell you, Braden?' Sam prodded, ignoring the other man.

Braden's face was a portrait of indecision. His thick, dirt-edged fingers clenched and loosened on the rifle as he struggled to make up his mind what he was going to do. He was acutely aware that all eyes were on him, that this tall, lean man was backing him into a corner and he was just letting it happen.

Matt watched his trigger-finger as it tightened and then relaxed, tightened and relaxed again and thought, *'All right, Sam, all right, you've pushed him far enough...*

'I'm warnin' you...' choked Braden, himself starting to sweat now.

Sam's eyes dared him to look away, but Braden was hooked, mesmerised by what he saw in their mild grey depths.

'I'll tell you,' Sam said, his voice a driving, compelling force. 'You're not doin' anythin' about it 'cause for the first time in your miserable life you're stoppin' to think about the consequences, ain't you, Braden? Thinkin' about what it's gonna be like to take another man's life. About whether or not you figure you could live with that afterwards.'

'I–'

'Go on,' urged Sam, slapping his chest again. 'There's one sure way to find out. *Try* it. But I'm gonna do you a favour, Braden. I'm gonna give you the piece of advice I wish someone'd given *me* before I killed *my* first man.

'It'll haunt you the rest of your days,' he said. 'An' you won't never truly get over it, 'cause it's a terrible, lastin' thing, an' once it's done, there ain't no undoin' it.' He fell silent and licked his lips. 'It'll be jus' the same with this feller Powell. You'll take him out of here an' down to the nearest tree, an' then you'll tie a rope around his neck an' get ready to hang him. An' you know what's gonna happen then, Braden?'

Almost against his will, the big miner shook his head slightly and croaked, 'N-no…'

'You're gonna look into his eyes,' Sam answered in a hiss. 'Jus' the way you're lookin' into my eyes now. An' you're gonna start wonderin' whether or not you'll be able to string him up like you said you would. An' it *will* be you, Braden. It won't be any of these other fellers. They'll all be lookin' to *you* to do it.

'Only by then you'll be thinkin' beyond the here an' now, you'll start thinkin' about afterwards, about how you're gonna get to sleep tonight, once it's all over, about how you'll keep seein' Powell's face ever' time you shut your eyes.

'In the mornin', a'course, things'll look better. You'll wake up an' tell yourself it was all just a nightmare. 'Cept that it wasn't. That feller'll still be hangin' right where you left him.'

Sam shook his head. 'Christ,' he said. 'I've known men who did what you're plannin' to do, plenty of 'em. But it never turned out like they thought it would. They never got over the way the other feller kicked or screamed as he choked, the way he messed his pants or how his tongue puffed up three times its size an' his eyes bugged out an' his face turned so dark it looked more like a rotten apple–'

Braden cracked his mouth open but didn't say anything. To fill the silence, Sam said, 'Now see sense, man. Back off, an' take these other fellers with you.'

It was asking the practically-impossible. Braden didn't move, didn't even blink. Matt watched his finger as it rested on the trigger, hardly daring to breathe. Did it tighten, or was that just a trick of the light?

Sam said, 'Braden? You hear me?'

Braden stared at him as sweat slid down his forehead.

'Braden, you might not think it right now, but I'm on your side, believe me.'

At last something seemed to leave the miner and he took the Henry away from Sam's chest and tossed it down into the slush at his feet.

'Aw hell,' he rumbled, turning away.

There were a few exclamations of surprise that he should have backed down without a fight, which didn't improve his mood one bit. Angrily he snapped to his followers, 'This business ain't worth the bother, I'm tellin' you! Now come on, it's cold out here an' I need another drink!'

He pushed through the crowd and they let him go, then closed in behind him and turned to follow him back up the street with a few sour, backward glances at the man who had deprived them of their evening's pleasure, the fellow called Zack tossing Colbert's .38 into the mud with open disgust before he turned away.

It was a long moment before Colbert stirred and went down into the street to retrieve the discarded weapons. 'That was either the bravest thing I've ever seen,' he remarked, 'or the most foolish.'

Sam raised his shoulders and let them

drop, weakening slightly at the knees as he finally allowed the tension to drain out of him. 'Well, I won't lay claim to no courage, marshal, but neither did my mama give birth to any idjits.'

Colbert watched the mob stamp back up the street, then turned his attention to the Texans and stuck out his free hand. 'Well, you helped us out of a hole there, no two ways about it. I'm Rance Colbert, by the way, and this here's my mother, Alice. Pleased to meet you.'

Matt nodded a greeting to the woman, but Sam went one better, lifting his hat to her and extending one hand. 'Ma'am. I'm only sorry you had to witness that there shameful exhibition. My name is–'

'We already know your name,' Alice Colbert interrupted, passing his carbine back to him. 'Lew Moffat has been singing your praises ever since the stage rolled in.' Glancing up at the snow-laden sky and tugging the shawl tighter around her shoulders, she said, 'Come inside before we all catch our deaths from this wretched weather.'

They followed her and her son into a spacious, low-ceilinged, well-lit cabin and Colbert closed the door behind them. It was without doubt the homeliest marshal's office Sam or Matt had ever seen. The room was as bright as a new pin. Everywhere they looked they saw signs of a woman's – Mrs Colbert's – influence. The office was still a place of business, serious law-enforcement business, but it was also surprisingly pleasant and comfortable.

Matt was impressed, but Sam, set in his ways, wasn't so sure. About the only thing missing was curtains at the windows, he thought sourly. For sure he reckoned that the bars of the cells in the jailhouse out back would be polished to a high and totally unnecessary sheen.

A black pot-bellied stove belched warm air into the room as Colbert gestured that their guests should pull up a couple of old ladderback chairs sitting against the far wall. As they went over there to get them, the Texans shucked their hats and gloves and unbuttoned their jackets.

'It's fortunate for us that you gentlemen happened along when you did,' Alice Colbert said, glancing at them over one shoulder as she busied herself at the stove.

Sam shrugged self-consciously. 'We like to do our bit to keep the peace, ma'am.'

'So I've heard.'

She took some mugs down from a row of neatly-spaced nails in the wall and, wrapping a cloth around the handle, she picked the pot up off the stove and started to fill them.

Colbert himself took off his hat, tossed it up onto the file cabinet beside the door, came around his big, polished desk and dropped into his chair. He had short, neatly-barbered fair hair, and in the pale lamp-light he looked tired and worn-down.

'I take it Judge Moffat told you what all of this is about?' he asked.

Sam nodded his thanks when Alice Colbert passed him a steaming mug. 'Only that someone was tryin' to fix it so's he wouldn't get to Little Cody for the trial.'

'Well, you're entitled to hear the whole of it, if you'd like. An explanation is the least we owe you,' Colbert said. He sat back and put his feet up on the desk, but as his mother came over and set a mug down beside him, she gestured that he should cut that out, and he set them down on the floor again.

'Go ahead, Rance,' said Matt. 'We're listening.'

The young marshal gave it to them short and sweet. 'Little Cody's a decent, peaceable town, but just like every other, it has its moments. I won't mince my words, gentlemen. My mother's heard it all before, and more than once, and I can assure you, she's not easily shocked.

'About three years ago, one of the Cypriots from Brady's saloon just along the way there was strangled to death up in the woods to the north of town. My father was the marshal here back then. He carried out an investigation of the crime, but to be frank with you, it was a pretty half-hearted affair.

Putting it bluntly, she was a whore, and who gives a cuss about the fate of a whore?

'Ten months later, another percentage girl went missing from Brady's. We didn't find her for a month. By then she was ... well, let's just say that she was a pretty enough girl when she was alive. After the coyotes had a go at her, she wasn't pretty any more. Near as we could tell, she'd been strangled as well, just like the other one.

'My father did as much as he could, but by then there wasn't a whole lot to go on, and it's a sad truth that whores die up and down the country every night of the week, for one reason or another. Now, don't misunderstand me. I'm not defending that view, I'm only saying it right out so that you'll understand why enquiries weren't as ... far-reaching, as maybe they could have been.

'We lost one more girl the same way, another Cypriot, last November. By then I was the marshal here and I didn't give a damn whether she was a saint or a sinner, she was a human being and no-one had the right to take her life the way they did. But I could've saved myself the trouble. I did the best job I could, but didn't turn up one single thing to help me find out who'd killed her.'

He took a pull at his coffee. 'Then, late one night about a fortnight ago, a young girl called Maureen Randall was beaten up and strangled to death in an alleyway about a block along from here. And that's where the killer made a bad mistake – he killed her *right here in town.*

'Just before she died, she sort of cried out, and that alerted some men who were leaving the restaurant right across the road. They came running just in time to see the killer rise up from over the body and take off down the alley.

'There was a chase, and they caught him. Turned out it was a feller by the name of Tom Powell. He said he'd found the girl's body and was trying to revive her when the other men turned up. According to him, he panicked and ran when they started yelling at him, afraid that they might accuse him of having killed her.'

'It *could* happen,' Matt murmured.

'Oh, sure,' Colbert allowed. 'But I know Tom Powell of old. He's just not the Good Samaritan type. And sure enough, when they fetched him down here and I emptied out his pockets, he had the entire contents of the girl's purse on him. He also had a cut across the knuckles of his right hand, where his fist might've snagged on the girl's teeth when he hit her. When Doc Burgess carried out the post mortem, he found that two of her front teeth had been snapped off.'

Sam sat forward. 'You folks mind if I smoke?' he asked.

Colbert said, 'Go ahead,' and his mother, who was on the other side of the office, taking her son's discarded hat and hanging it up on a peg in back of the door, immediately came back over, took an ashtray off Colbert's desk and handed it to him.

Sam said, 'I take it this girl Maureen Randall wasn't a, uh, prostitute?'

'That's right. Oh, I'm not saying she was an angel, but she was a good enough girl, just sixteen years old. Losing her just ruined her folks. That's why local feeling's running so high – why we're starting to have scenes like the one you broke up for us just now.'

Sam bit the end off his cigar and spat it into the ashtray, then struck a match and finally got the thing alight. 'Who's this Tom Powell I been defendin'?'

Alice took over the narrative. 'His folks run a roadhouse about fifteen miles west of here. You likely passed it on your way in.'

'We did, ma'am. An' now I'm thinkin' I understand why the driver of that there coach was so darn set on us goin' right by without stoppin'.'

'The Powells have never been what you would call model citizens,' Alice went on. 'There's old Nathan Powell, a harsh and venal man if ever I saw one, his wife, 'Becca, his sons – Tom's brothers – Saul and Jed – and his daughter Eve and her husband, Lije Tucker. Although we've got no proof of it, we've heard that sometimes riders travelling alone never come out of that roadhouse once they've gone in, leastways not alive, and I for one have no reason to doubt it.'

Colbert drank some more of his coffee. 'When I explained the situation to Judge Moffat, he was of the opinion that it was Saul and Jed who tried to scare him off last night and today. For sure, I wouldn't put it past them. Old Nathan's already been to town to tell me how "wise" it would be for me to drop the case. He's claiming that Tom's innocent, and that he won't get a fair shake of the stick here in Little Cody because he's a Powell.

'Maybe he's right. Folks around here hate the Powells like poison, mostly because they're afraid of them. But Tom Powell killed that girl, and all the others, I'm sure. They're all prone to violence, but Tom … he's kind of sick in the head. He really *likes* hurting people.'

'They sound like real fine pillars of the community,' Matt said grimly.

'They are, Mr Dury–'

'Matt.'

Colbert nodded. 'Matt. I tell you, I'll just be glad when this whole business is over and done with.'

Alice said, 'It might have been over and done with a lot sooner than we expected, if you gentlemen hadn't taken a hand. I don't care what you say to the contrary, Mr Judge. It was a very courageous thing you did out there.'

'Aw, I'm an old lawdog from way back, ma'am,' Sam explained, rising to his feet and picking up his Spencer. 'Anyway, I guess we better be movin' along. We're pullin' out in the mornin', so it's best we get an early night tonight. But I sure hope things work out for you folks.' He offered his hand to Colbert. 'So long, Rance. From what I've seen of you, you're doin' a fine job around here.'

A sour smiled touched Colbert's mouth. 'For my age, you mean?' he asked caustically.

'Rance!'

Sam's cordiality cooled a little. 'I meant no offence, son.'

Colbert dropped his shoulders and looked sheepish. 'And none taken, Mr Judge. Forgive me. I'm afraid that ever since my father ... that is to say, since I took over from my father, I've had these "tender years" of mine thrown up in my face time and again by those folks who don't think I'm up to the job. I guess I'm starting to get a little sensitive about it.'

'Well, I'll tell you this much. I couldn't've faced down that mob the way you did when *I* was your age.'

Colbert's smile was warmer this time. 'That's quite a compliment coming from "The Pistol Prince" himself.'

Sam winced. 'Son,' he said, tipping the cigar in his mouth so that it pointed at the ceiling. 'You just put your finger on the one thing *I'm* a little sensitive about, so I guess that makes us even.' He nodded to Alice. 'So long, ma'am. Rance. Thanks for the coffee.'

They let themselves out into the full night

just as a fresh scattering of snow began to descend from the heavens.

One look down into the street next morning confirmed the worst. More snow had fallen during the night, a lot of it. Tin chimneys puffed smoke into the dull, breezy sky. Icicles hung like daggers and dirks from every ledge and sill.

Shivering, Sam said, 'Dammit.'

He glanced across the room at the bed in the corner. Hearing him up and about, Matt stirred beneath the covers. 'Is it that bad?' he asked in a muffled croak.

'It's *worse*.'

The room was cold and Sam dressed hurriedly. He had to crack a thin layer of ice in the wash basin before he could soap his face and shave. He hated the cold, more so as he got older, and the prospect of wintering up here when he'd been counting on riding south filled him with a sense of injustice.

Still, he had no choice in the matter. Time was when he'd have chanced making the ride out and to hell with the weather, but he was older now, crowding fifty, and Lord, he felt it. Likewise, his roan, Charlie, was no longer a youngster. And one last look outside, at the low, dark clouds, convinced him that any attempt to leave town would surely be interrupted partway through by another blizzard. Given the option, he'd as soon be trapped up here than out in the surrounding, lonely wastes.

After Matt stirred himself, they got wrapped up and ready to quit the hotel and go get some breakfast. When they opened the door, however, they found Mitzi waiting for them with a good morning meow.

Sam bent, picked the fat tan and white cat up and ruffled the loose fur between her ears. She felt cold and looked worn out after a night on the town. He put her on the bed he'd slept in and, picking up his scent and what little body heat still remained in the rumpled sheets, she quickly burrowed under the covers, pausing just once to blink lazily at him, meow some more and run her small pink tongue up across her whiskers.

Sam nodded his understanding. 'I'll fetch you somethin' to eat just as soon as I can,' he promised solemnly.

Although it was still relatively early, Little Cody was already starting to look lively. But as they set off towards the restaurant, their attention was quickly taken by two muffled riders who had just come in from the west and were scattering foot-travellers in their haste to get down to the marshal's office.

Pausing, Sam and Matt looked them over as they reined in on the other side of the snow-choked street. The fellow with the longish, red-fair hair was about twenty five or so, his features rounded and not unpleasant, his skin pale and freckled, his eyes green and his build and height average. He wore the collar of his sheepskin jacket turned up and his hat pulled low, but as he dismounted they got a glimpse of the left side of his face, and it was sore-looking and bruised – where Judge Moffat had clobbered him with his cane.

This was Jed Powell, then.

The man with him was shorter and broader, with a Saltillo blanket draped poncho-style over his thick jacket and his flat-brimmed black hat worn at an angle over his thick, curly black hair. He was about thirty, awkward with the bulk of his arms and legs, moon-faced, with pale blue eyes, a hooked nose and a shaggy goatee beard.

Sam felt Matt's eyes on him, and guessing what was in his mind, he nodded. This would be Lije Tucker, Tom Powell's brother-in-law.

The two men went bulling into Rance Colbert's office without bothering to knock. Their horses waited patiently for them with hanging heads and trailing reins. The animals looked poor and ill-used, broken, not gentled, to the saddle.

'You figure maybe we ought to go over there?' asked Matt.

Sam shook his head. 'No. I doubt if they're here to make trouble. 'Sides, I'd hate to make a habit of hornin' in on Colbert's business.'

'Yeah, he *was* a mite touchy, wasn't he?' Matt agreed.

'He's young. Folks keep tellin' him he's *too* young. Maybe even his ma. You see the way she tidied up after him las' night?'

Matt nodded. 'He needs a chance to prove himself.'

'So we'll stay out of it, if we can.'

A moment later Jed and Lije Tucker came back out into the street, took up their reins and swung aboard their mounts, then rode on up the street with nary a sideways glance. But they looked mad enough to kick a bobcat. Rance had evidently sent them out of there with a flea in their collective ear.

The Texans continued on to the restaurant, where Sam's mood brightened a bit once he had some food inside him, but only fractionally. Matt could see it in the moody way he chewed on his first cigar of the day, the way he constantly ranged his eyes across the sky beyond the window, searching vainly for some small glimmer of sunlight, a sign that the weather might not break down completely after all.

Outside, the town suddenly started buzzing with expectation. Curious, Sam and Matt twisted around to see why. The law office door had swung open and a tall, hawk-faced man with rumpled red-fair hair and a long, sharp nose came out onto the street, his hands shackled behind him.

Rance Colbert followed him out, a shotgun cradled in the crook of his right arm, his mother, still grasping her shawl, right behind him. With a shove in the shoulder, Rance finally got his prisoner – Tom Powell – moving.

Alice Colbert watched them go with a worried chew at her lower lip. Some of the other diners actually got up and gathered at the window to watch as the killer was marched up the street. Outside, passers-by had also stopped to watch.

This was the first chance Sam and Matt had had to see the man who had caused all the fuss. Near as they could tell, he looked unremarkable, just another unwashed troublemaker. Tom was over thirty, but not by much. He swaggered up the street with all the disdain of the supremely confident. When he smiled, as he did, insolently, to all the people they passed, he revealed discoloured, snaggle-edged teeth.

What struck the Texans most, however, was the silence that overtook the street. Normally a man as reviled as this here Powell would have had insults thrown at him, and maybe a few missiles as well. But as Colbert shoved him again to keep him going, no-one uttered a word, they just stood and looked, morbidly fascinated by this woman-killer, and the silence which extended itself into the restaurant as well was a palpable, frightened thing.

Sam turned to the man sitting across from him at the trestle table. 'What's the occasion?'

The man was malnourished and nervous-looking, dressed in a town suit and an emerald-green cravat. 'Haven't you heard?' he asked. 'Tom Powell's trial starts at ten o'clock this mornin'.'

'Whereabouts?'

'The municipal hall.'

Matt glanced thoughtfully at his companion. 'Want to see justice in action?' he asked.

Sam pushed his empty plate aside. 'Won't be nothin' worth seein' this mornin'. Jury'll be sworn in. Defence an' prosecution'll do some speechifyin' to set the mood. This afternoon it might pick up.'

'All right. This afternoon.'

They finished their meal, left some money tucked under their plates and went back out onto the street. Sam bought some scraps from the local meat market and smuggled them up to their room for the ravenous Mitzi, and then he and Matt went into the first saloon they came to, which was warm and practically deserted, and drank coffee by the gallon. There wasn't a whole lot else you could do in Little Cody, if you were just passing through.

The morning ended. Folks began to appear out on the street again, coming back down from the municipal hall, which was a big frame building up at the farthest end of town.

The first man to enter the saloon and belly up to the bar was a pot-bellied sixty year-old with a stiff leg and a bushy white beard.

'What's been happenin' up there?' asked the bartender as he filled a shot glass and scraped the old-timer's money up off the counter.

The old-timer pulled a face. 'Aw, nothin' much, to date. Jury was sworn in, an' after that there was just a lot of speechifyin'.'

At the corner table, Sam winked at his partner and said in a stage whisper, 'What'd I tell you?'

It was just a little after noon, and evidently court was due to convene again at one. When the clock on the wall behind the bar said a quarter to, a few of the lunchtime drinkers began to slip away.

Sam and Matt went out into the raw, blustery day with them, and when they entered the municipal hall, the temperature hardly lifted. Basically, the municipal hall was a barn-like structure in which local wing-dings and occasional meetings were held. A dozen chairs had been set out for the jury in two rows of six along the left-hand wall, and a table sat directly ahead, facing the desks that had been positioned for use by the defence and prosecution. Taking up much of the rest of the hall were the jumble of chairs and stools that had been set out for the public on either side of a makeshift aisle.

People were already milling around when they arrived – including Al Braden and a few other miners – finding and claiming the best seats, and the jury-men were likewise starting to take their places, although there were still a few empty spaces visible. Hand-cuffed to a chair directly opposite the jury sat Tom Powell, and directly behind him, Rance Colbert lounged against the wall, the shotgun – now broken open – still nestled in the bend of his arm.

Sam and Matt sat at the back of the hall, near the door. A glimpse of fair hair caught Sam's eye and he noticed Alice Colbert walk past and take a seat in the front row. Glancing around, he saw no sign of Jed Powell or his stocky, blocky brother-in-law.

The men who would be arguing for or against the defendant turned up. One was a sassy-looking young man in a pearl grey suit. Sam asked the woman sitting next to him who the fellow was, and she said he was Alvin Clark, an attorney from Cloud Peak who'd been engaged by the Powells. The prosecutor was a local school superintendent named Bob Robbins, who'd been studying law by mail for six months.

Slowly some kind of order began to settle over the temporary courtroom. At exactly one o'clock, a door in the back wall opened and Judge Moffat came through, looking grim in his heavy black broadcloth. As he shuffled to the table, still leaning heavily on his cane, Rance Colbert straightened up and called out, *'All rise.'*

Everyone apart from Tom Powell stood up and remained standing until the judge had seated himself. Then, as the townsfolk resumed their seats, Rance went over to the judge and bent to whisper something to him.

A few of the locals coughed and shuffled about, getting themselves comfortable. Up at the bench, Lew Moffat was joined by counsel. Around them, townspeople started muttering impatiently. Someone sneezed. Lew Moffat glanced at the jury, then back to Rance, then nodded.

Once counsel were back in their seats, he reached for the gavel on the desk and struck it three times to being the court to order. Addressing the jury, he said, 'There are three of you missing, including your elected foreman. Do any of you know where they are?'

Head-shakes met the judge's question.

The judge took out his pocket watch and looked at it for a long moment before snapping it shut. 'I might as well tell you before we go any further that I do not tolerate poor time-keeping when court's in session. However, the weather being how it is, we'll give the missing men another five minutes, but if it happens again while I'm here, I'll be considering fines for the offenders.'

A low babble rose up. Three minutes ticked by and still there was no sign of the three missing jurors. Alvin Clark went up to the judge and did some more whispering. A couple of minutes later the judge banged his gavel again and announced, 'Defence moves that, in the continued absence of the complete jury, I suspend this hearing for the remainder of the day. Does counsel for the prosecution have any objections?'

Bob Robbins, a tall, angular, bookish man with glasses, rose and said, 'No objections, Your Honour – but may I move to suggest that Marshal Colbert finds out just what has happened to the missing men without further delay?'

The judge nodded. 'Good idea.' Addressing

the assembly as a whole, he said, 'Court will convene again at ten o'clock sharp tomorrow morning.'

As soon as the judge made his pronouncement, Alice Colbert sprang up out of her chair and hurried towards the bench. The rest of the townsfolk had already started speculating darkly as they crowded into the aisle and rushed to get out of the cold hall and back to their snug, warm homes or places of business in order to discuss this new development in greater detail and comfort.

Matt glanced sideways at his partner. Up at the bench, the judge, Rance, his mother, Alvin Clark and Bob Robbins had their heads together in agitated conversation, while Tom Powell lounged confidently in his chair, eyeing the fidgety jurors with a smirk on his angular, pale face.'

'Don't much care for the sound of this, do you?' asked Matt.

Sam looked serious. 'Uh-huh.'

'You figure it's time to buy in again?'

With a fatalistic sigh, Sam stood up. 'Hell,

we been buyin' in ever since we first saw the judge takin' lumps down in that alley, ain't we?'

Pushing through the departing crowd, they started up towards the judge's bench.

FIVE

Lifting their hats to Alice Colbert, the Texans came to a halt and Sam said, 'Anythin' we can do to help, Rance?'

Everyone up there turned around to look at them. Rance considered for a moment, then threw a glance over his shoulder at his prisoner and said, 'Well ... I guess I'd appreciate it if you could swing by and check on the missing jurors for me while I take Tom back down to the jailhouse.'

'Sure. Who are they, an' where do they live?'

Before Rance could reply, Alvin Clark cut in. 'And who might you be?' he asked imperiously.

Sam eyed him sternly, but it was Alice who responded. 'This is Sam Judge, the famous town-tamer, and his associate, Matt Dury,' she said primly. 'And I will thank you to show them a little more respect in future, Mr Clark.'

Recognition of their names showed in Clark's dark, duplicitous eyes. 'Oh yes – the men who foiled that stagecoach robbery yesterday.'

'Robbery had nothin' to do with it, son,' said Sam. 'As you very well know.'

Clark stiffened. 'What do you mean by that?'

'Gentlemen,' said Judge Moffat. 'This isn't getting us anywhere – and time may be of the essence.'

Matt glanced at Rance. 'What are their names and where can we find 'em?' he prodded.

'Will Lawrence lives above the sign works. That's just along the street a-ways, next door to Bonner's Dry Goods.'

'I'm on my way.'

As Matt turned and headed out after the last of the departing townsfolk, the young marshal went on, 'John Miller lives on Allen

Road. That's just behind—'

'Never mind directions, Rance,' said his mother briskly. 'I know where it is. Mr Judge and I can go together.'

Rance nodded. 'All right. I'll go see what's become of Hec Courtwright as soon as I've got Tom safely back behind bars.'

Sam and the woman left the hall behind them and waded across the morass of churned snow and slush that was Main. The afternoon was dark and the wind cut like the blade of a Bowie knife. Once, in her haste, Alice almost slipped and Sam reached out to take her arm and steady her. In that moment of unexpected closeness, she looked up at him with some embarrassment and blushed like a schoolgirl.

As they continued on, Sam decided to do a little fishing. 'I didn't see your husband in court, ma'am,' he remarked innocuously.

Without looking at him she said, 'My husband is … no longer with us.'

'Aw, my condolences. I didn't mean to open up old wounds—'

'Please don't concern yourself. I'm over it now.'

She led them into a sidestreet that lifted beneath them to reach a wooded ridge along which had been built a row of thick-walled log cabins. With a little self-conscious laugh she said, 'It's silly, I know, but I'm afraid I just can't help thinking the worst.'

He steered her around a puddle of ice and growled, 'Sometimes it pays to fear the worst.'

About mid-way along the block, Alice turned onto a cleared path, went up to a door and knocked.

There was no response.

She knocked again. They waited, shifting around in their cold anxiety. Still there was no answer. Sam balled up one gloved fist and thumped heavily against the door. At last it opened a crack and a short, balding man of about thirty-five stuck his bloodless, tired face cautiously into the gap. His dark eyes travelled quickly from Sam to Alice, then dropped so that they wouldn't have to meet the woman's face. 'Oh, Mrs Colbert...'

Alice glanced up at Sam, then turned her attention to the juror, John Miller, and said, 'Is ... is there anything wrong, John? We were wondering why you didn't turn up for the trial this afternoon.'

He made a fussy little gesture that was meant to convey that he'd been too busy to bother with that. 'Ah, yeah, I ... I'm sorry about that. But ... well, the wife was taken sick, an' you know how it is, I got three young kids...'

Sam, not believing a word of it, reached up and shoved the door inwards, and Miller staggered back into the cabin. A crackling fire kept the place warm. Two children, both girls, were sitting on a rug with a couple of carved wooden toys in their laps, watching him through big, uneasy eyes.

Sam looked around. There was no-one else in the room. He spotted a likely–looking door and headed for it. Miller grabbed him by the arm and said indignantly, 'Hey now, who–?' Sam pushed him away and continued across the room with Alice at his heels, objecting, 'Really, Mr Judge, you have no right to–'

Sam opened the door. It swung into a small bedroom. There wasn't space in there for much more than the brass-framed double bed and cot, in which a chubby, bald baby was sleeping and making little gurgling noises.

Sam went in, edged around the bed and drew back the curtain at the small, square oilpaper window. Darkness was immediately transformed into semi-darkness.

A woman, presumably Miller's wife, was resting in the bed, her long black hair fanned out on the striped pillow beneath her. She had been sleeping. Now she opened her glazed eyes and gave a little moan, then writhed under the blankets, clearly in distress.

'…who-who…?'

Sam winced, sucking his breath in through his teeth. Alice made a sound of anguish in her throat and hurried around the other side of the bed to take the woman's hand. 'Oh, Freda! Whatever have they done to you?'

Sam turned to Miller. There was no surprise in him, for he'd been anticipating something like this. But there *was* fury – fury at the kind of men who could hit women, not once but many times. He wanted to raise his voice, but mindful of the children he kept it down.

'Taken sick, you said? What kind of sickness is it that leaves a woman lookin' like she jus' went five rounds with Gentleman Jim Corbett?'

Miller flustered and glanced down at the baby sleeping in the cot. 'I … she took a tumble–'

'*I'll* say she took a tumble!' Sam came over, put a hand on Miller's chest and forced him out of the room. He followed the man out and closed the door behind him, leaving Alice to tend to the beaten woman. Crowding Miller close, he said, 'They scared you off, didn't they?'

'I–'

'Which one did it, Miller? Jed Powell or Lije Tucker? Or was it both?'

For a moment he felt nothing but loathing for this balding, tired-looking man. How could he have stood by and watched them beat his wife the way they had? But then reason returned and he reminded himself that the world was made up of hawks and doves, that the Powells were a faction of hawks, that Miller and men like him were and always would be doves.

Sighing, feeling the anger leaving him, he said, 'How long ago were they here?'

Miller clung stubbornly to his story. 'I don't know what–'

'How long!'

That was all it took to make him cave in. 'I don't know. About an hour.'

'Who did it?'

Miller looked down at the rug under his feet, fighting tears. 'Lije Tucker. He was already here, waitin' for me when I got back from the municipal hall at noon.'

'Would you stand up an' say that in court?'

Miller's moist eyes came up to his face again. 'N-no.'

'I didn't think so.' Reaching a decision he said, 'Miller, you better go find a doctor for your wife while Mrs Colbert's here to watch your kids.'

When the man still stood there, un-moving, he hissed, *'Do it!'*

That snapped some life back into him and he hustled over to the antler-horn coat-rack and took down his overcoat. Alice came out of the bedroom, her eyes red-rimmed. Seeing Sam about to head for the door, she put a hand on his arm and asked, 'What are you going to do?'

'Find Matt, see what's happened to the other jurors.'

'And then?'

'Go after Jed Powell an' Lije Tucker,' he said.

'Be careful then, Mr Judge. Don't do anything rash. The Powells are as cunning as snakes.'

He looked down into her very handsome face, genuinely surprised. 'I thank you for your concern, ma'am, I surely do.'

Miller was crouching over his girls, telling them to be good for Mrs Colbert while he was gone. Sam went past him, opened the front door and went outside. It was a slippery walk back down to Main, like trying to walk on grease, but once there it became easier because most of the storekeepers had cleared the snow away from the storefronts, heaping it into knobbly embankments three feet high along the edge of the street.

He saw Matt just leaving the sign works and striding down to the marshal's office. There was a break in the wagon traffic and he hurried across the best way he could. Once he reached the other side he called Matt's name, and when Matt turned around, the look on his face told him everything.

'Jed Powell paid your man a visit, am I right?' he asked as he came up, puffing out vapour.

Matt nodded. 'Him and Tucker both paid

Lawrence's pa a visit sometime this morning, near as I can figure it. The old man's touching seventy. They roughed him up, wrecked the parlour and told him to tell Lawrence that worse would happen if he didn't quit the jury rightaway.'

Sam spat off to the side. 'An a'course, Lawrence's too damn' scared to make a complaint?' he muttered angrily.

'Well, you can hardly blame him. To hear him tell it, his pa's the only thing he's got in the world.'

Sam reached into his jacket for a cigar, bit the end off and spat it away, telling himself to calm down. All right. So no-one was prepared to buck the Powells. He clapped Matt on the arm. 'Let's get down to the marshal's office an' see how Colbert got on.'

Rance had found pretty much what Sam and Matt had already found before him – another clear-cut case of intimidation, and a scared man who not only refused to go on serving on the jury, but who had also been warned – forcibly – against making any form of complaint against his tormentor, Jed Powell.

As he finished his account, Rance snatched up his shotgun and said grimly, 'Now, if you gents'll excuse me...'

'Ridin' out to the Powell place, son?'

'Uh-huh. Oh, I can't arrest 'em, I know that. But I can damn' sure tell 'em what they can expect if they go on trying to scare our jurors.'

Sam struck a match and got the cigar alight. 'Might be best if *we* go, Rance.'

Without warning, the lawman bristled. 'I hope you're not trying to say I'm too young for the job, Judge. I'm grateful for your help, of course I am, but–'

'Whoa, there,' Sam cut in. 'All I'm sayin' is them Powells know you'll be comin' after 'em when you find out what they did here. They'll be expectin' you. Might even be fixin' to ambush you.'

'Oh, come *on* now–'

'In this kind of weather, you could disappear and nobody'd ever be able to tie it to the Powells, not for sure,' Matt said seriously. 'And with you out of the way, they could just ride in and set Tom free any time they liked, and there'd be no-one to stop them.'

Colbert smiled coldly. '*You'd* stop them, I suspicion.' Just as suddenly he sobered and shook his head. 'No. I know you mean well but… Heck, this is my job, Mr Judge. It's what I get *paid* for. Meaning no disrespect, I can't just stand by and allow you to take the law into your own hands.'

'Well, at least take one of us with you,' Matt argued. 'Tell you what. If it'll make you feel any happier, make it official. Deputise us.'

'*Deputise* you?'

'We're already drawing deputies' wages from Constable Mitchell,' Matt told him. 'We might as well have the badge that goes with it.'

Rance considered the idea. At length the lines on his youthful face eased a little as a fleeting smile touched his mouth. He put the shotgun down, went across to his desk, opened it and rooted through a drawer, then took out a star, which he tossed to Matt.

'Consider yourself deputised,' he said. Turning to Sam he raised an eyebrow. 'Will you watch the store for me while I'm gone, Mr Judge?'

'Sure.'

'Thanks. Matt – better get your horse saddled and ready to ride.'

Matt finished pinning the star to the front of his brush jacket, then threw a wink at his partner before turning his attention to the marshal. 'Meet you out front in ten minutes,' he replied. *'Boss.'*

The Powell roadhouse lay about fifteen miles outside of town. The horses floundered through the belly-high snow in a tortuous leap-and-stop gait. Ninety minutes into the ride, fresh snow started falling again, and they turned the animals off the trail and into some sheltering trees.

'Damn this weather!' said Rance, reaching back into one saddlebag. 'And damn those Powells!'

He fetched out a small silver flask, flipped up the top and took a snort, then passed it to Matt. Matt sniffed at the neck, identified brandy and took a pull of his own. At once the alcohol warmed him through.

As he snapped the flask shut again, he noticed that something had been engraved on it, and tilting it to the watery daylight, he read: TO TOWN MARSHAL VERNON COLBERT – IN APPRECIATION OF TEN YEARS OF LOYAL PUBLIC SERVICE – FROM ALL YR FRIENDS IN LITTLE CODY – 11th OCTOBER 1880.

He passed it back and said, 'I guess your dad must've been quite a lawman.'

Rance's shoulders moved under his coat in a dismissive gesture. 'He was. Towards the finish, though, he … well, let's just say he had other things on his mind.' He stuffed the flask away and squinted out at the steadily-falling snow. 'I'm, ah, sorry I blew up at your friend earlier on, Matt.'

'Forget it. Sam probably has.' Matt indicated the trail with a jerk of the chin. 'Well, what's it to be, marshal – press on or go back?'

'Press on. We've come this far.'

They urged the horses back onto the trail and ploughed doggedly forward. The mountains were trapped in a snow-shaker that had been thoroughly and viciously agitated. Thirty minutes later, with the trail ahead leading between two low, aspen-covered hills and their destination no more than a mile further on, the deep bark of a long gun suddenly tore across the dismal, windswept afternoon and snow burst up in a miniature explosion about a dozen feet ahead of them.

Matt's pony reared up in surprise, and Rance's sorrel broke stride and started prancing sideways. But although the men themselves were aching from the hard, pro-longed ride, they'd been preparing them-selves for a confrontation at journey's-end, and now their reaction was both instinctive and immediate.

Kicking the horses to speed, they dragged

their handguns from leather and returned fire on the move.

Flame winked from in among the quaking aspens on the ridge to their right, so they concentrated their fire in that direction. The hidden bushwhacker triggered back once more, but with snow tumbling around them like pale autumn leaves, his shot went wide.

Matt and Rance charged on for about ten yards, ignoring the folly of trying to move so fast in such treacherous conditions. For a moment all was confusion – gunfire, the thunder of horse-hooves, the tormented howl of the wind, the flicker and bite of the snow. Then Rance's sorrel lost its footing and crashed sideways, spilling the marshal himself out of his saddle and into a drift.

Matt emptied his Tranter into the trees, wanting to look back but not daring to. His pony lumbered into the narrow pass, snow bursting up from under its pumping legs like spray flying back off the prow of a ship.

Another spit of flame through the spiralling snow. Another rifle shot booming out of the blizzard. Matt ducked low over his horse's powerful neck, shoving the empty gun back into leather, switching his reins from his left hand to his right, then pulling the left-side Tranter free.

One more shot roared through the overcast. Matt turned the pony around in an eruption of snow, and the animal gave a high, scared scream. For one desperate moment he saw only a jumble of images – sky, snow, timber, brush, his horse's flying mane. He nearly came unseated as the animal twisted around to face their attacker but somehow held on.

Then he saw another spot of flame tear from the rifleman's weapon and he triggered three shots back at him, firing in blind desperation, and trusting as much to luck as skill.

Something moved up there in the aspen shadows – the bushwhacker's rifle skittered down through the snow, dark against the white background.

A man followed it down.

He tumbled out of a clump of hawthorn bushes, moving like a bag of rags. He started off head-first, then twisted to the side and rolled another few yards. After that he lost some of his momentum and dragged to a stop part-way down the slope, snow powdering his brightly-coloured poncho.

Silence but for the howling wind claimed the pass. Matt listened hard, just in case the dead man had fetched some company along with him. He ranged his gunmetal-grey eyes up across the snowy slopes.

Nothing.

He dismounted and tugged his pony over to the side of the trail. Spooked, the horse didn't want to go. Finally he tied the animal to some brush, then broke into a plunging, high-stepping run back the way he'd come.

'Rance?'

There was no response. But twenty yards further on he was relieved to see the young lawman and his jumpy horse both struggling up out of the snow, Rance irritably brushing himself down and inspecting the sorrel for any sign of injury.

Slowing, Matt called, 'You all right?'

Rance turned and threw him an impatient wave. Clearly the fall had dented his pride, if nothing else. 'Did you get him?' he countered shortly.

'Uh-huh.'

'Kill him?'

'Uh-huh.'

'Damn.' Irascibly he kicked at the snow. 'Who was it?'

'From the looks of his poncho, I'd say Lije Tucker.'

The lawman pondered that. 'Well,' he concluded, 'if ever a bastard had it coming, he was the one, I guess.'

Matt went back through the pass, cutting an angle up across the slope towards the body. Already it was partially covered by snow. Matt approached it cautiously. When he was close enough, he toed the man over onto his back.

He was right. It *was* Lije Tucker, and he *was* dead.

He knelt beside the corpse, flipping the poncho-style Saltillo blanket up so that it covered the dead man's staring eyes. Two bullets had struck Lije in the body, one high up, about six inches above his left nipple, the other dead-centre of the breastbone. Now the front of his jacket was soggy with blood, and the snow upon which he had come to rest was a slushy, watery pink.

Straightening, he climbed further up the slope and into the trees. It wasn't difficult to find the spot where Lije had staked himself out. The embers of a small, smokeless fire still glowed faintly in the gusting wind, and a dented old coffee pot sitting on a rock at the fire's edge still puffed steam into the cold air.

Thoughtfully Matt reached up and fingered the badge pinned to the front of his jacket. It looked as if he'd been right to warn Rance about the possibility of an ambush. Anticipating a visit from the local law, the Powells must have posted Lije to watch the trail out from Little Cody and take any action he considered appropriate when it finally showed up. These tin stars of theirs hadn't been anything more to him than targets.

He pushed through the tangled under-growth and found the dead man's poorly-used horse. As he led the animal down the slope, he wondered how the Powells were going to react when they found out about their dead in-law.

Together he and the marshal hoisted Lije up across his saddle and tied him in place. The horse balked at the idea of carrying a corpse, as horses always do. Eventually the snow eased up a bit and they were able to dry off their saddles, swing up and continue on their way.

The threat of early darkness was already stealing into the afternoon sky by the time the scattering of snow-capped log buildings came into sight. As they rode the last twenty yards towards the roadhouse, the door opened slowly and the Powells filed out to watch their approach.

Nathan ... 'Becca ... Jed...

And then—

The girl who came out last of all was tall and slim and in her early twenties. There were no prizes for guessing that she was Eve Tucker, Lije's wife. She wore a dark, starched dress. Under any other circumstances she would have been breathtakingly beautiful, no two ways about. She had large, almond-shaped green eyes, an agreeable tilt to her small, freckled nose and an undeniably sensual mouth. Her pale, now emotionless face was framed by long, copper-coloured hair.

She saw the burden packed across Lije's horse and must have guessed its identity, but she gave no reaction as she came to stand beside her kin, she just stood there with her breasts rising and falling as she sucked in air, her dark dress darkened still further by the damp snow, her hands clenched into fists, her eyes showing distrust and guile.

Finally Matt and Rance reined down and sat their horses silently before the Powells, mirroring their appraisal.

Nathan Powell was a big, blocky man of

about fifty summers. He had restless green eyes and the kind of nose they usually saddled wooden Indians with. There were a few greying whiskers sprouting and curling around his thick lips. His reddish hair was lightening to grey and he wore it swept back from a long, nut-brown face to gather and curl at the nape of his neck.

He wore a plain hickory shirt and grey pants tucked into knee-high black boots. He didn't say a word at first. He seemed not to notice the biting cold. Then he used the Winchester he was holding to gesture towards the body.

'You killed Lije,' he said in a low, soft voice that was totally at odds with his appearance.

The wind picked up, then died.

Matt nudged his pony forward and passed the reins of the death-horse down to Jed. 'I killed him,' he replied.

'*Bastard!*' Eve hissed through grinding teeth. She tried to snatch Jed's Colt out of its holster but he thrust her away from him and swore at her to hold still. Muttering another filthy word, she glared up at Matt like a savage animal, her shoulders lifting and dropping to the rhythm of her swift, frenzied breathing.

'I'm sorry, ma'am,' Matt said, addressing her directly. 'For you. But not for Lije. Any man who'd do the things he did today deserves everything he's got coming.'

'That's a hell of a thing to say to a woman you just widowed!' snarled the girl's mother.

Matt put his eyes on her. 'Becca Powell was a big barrel of a woman, also in her fifties. She wasn't just big with fat, although there was plenty of that, but also with muscle, thick slabs of it. She had very fine, very dry grey hair and a cruel, grudge-toting look to her round, pocked face. The fact that she didn't have any teeth gave her head a weird, hollow look. She carried a Colt that was slightly smaller than a canyon in her right fist, and it was obvious that the woman and the weapon were no strangers.

She said, 'You come out here, kill my son-in-law for no good reason–'

'Lije died because he tried to bushwhack us,' Rance cut in sternly. He eyed the Powells with a frown, then asked suddenly, 'Where's Saul, by the way?'

Something subtle and foxy came into Nathan's shifty green eyes and he said flatly, 'Saul?'

'I don't see him around. He inside?'

'He ain't here,' said 'Becca.

'Gone to get that shoulder of his seen to, I guess,' said Matt.

With studied ignorance 'Becca said, 'What're you gabbin' about, mister? What shoulder?'

Rance looked beyond them, to the blank roadhouse windows, searching. He was in no mood to play games. He just wanted to say what he'd come here to say, and then get back to town. Leaning forward in the saddle, he nodded. 'All right. We'll take your word for it that Saul's not here. That's too bad, because I've got a message for him, and for all the rest of you, too. You know why we're here, Nathan. Your boys've been cutting up rough again, beating up Judge Moffat, holding up the eastbound stage, intimidating the jurors at Tom's trial.' He shifted his weight. 'Well, enough's enough. It's got to stop. If it doesn't, I'll be back to arrest the whole pack of you.'

'You got no authority around here, Colbert,' Nathan said in his quiet, slightly menacing voice. 'You can't threaten us.' With a twitch of the Winchester he added, 'Best you turn around an' leave afore I lose my temper.'

'We're going,' Rance replied. 'But I mean it, Nathan. You people might think you're above the law, but I'm here to tell you you're not. Tom'll have his day in court. There's nothing you can do to change it – so don't even try.'

He shortened his rein, touched his heels to his sorrel's flanks and backed the horse away from the roadhouse. Matt followed his example, keeping his eyes on the Powells the whole time. The horses shushed back through the churned snow until there was a gap of about thirty yards between them.

'You won't get away with what you done to Lije!' Eve yelled with a spiteful jab of one long fingernail. 'I'll kill you for that myself, mister!'

Looking back at her, feeling her fury, Matt didn't doubt it. As they finally turned the horses and kicked them back into that ball-busting leap-and-stop gait, he was fully expecting a bullet or two to chase them on their way.

SIX

'More coffee, Mr Judge?' asked Alice Colbert.

Sam looked up at the woman from his seat behind Rance's desk and shook his head. 'No thank you, ma'am.'

'Are you sure? It's still piping hot.'

'I'm sure, thank you all the same.'

Alice's smile was just a tic in the muscles that worked her mouth as she moved away from the stove with her own refilled mug in hand. 'I'm sorry,' she said. 'That must be about the twentieth time I've asked you that since I got here.'

She'd arrived at the office about four hours earlier, having finished assisting the local doctor in patching up Miller's wife and then visiting the Powells' other victims to check on their injuries. She had shown sur-

167

prise when she'd first found Sam looking after the office, but then anxiety had taken over once he told her where her son had gone.

Since then, Alice had wandered restlessly around the office, finding all kinds of fiddly little inconsequential things to occupy her mind, punctuating each of them regularly with a look out the window into the dark, snowy evening.

At first Sam had tried to calm her fears. It was a long ride out to the Powell place and back. The weather had likely slowed Rance and Matt down. They might have decided to hole up someplace till the worst of the snow had fallen.

But all his attempts to console her had fallen on deaf ears. As she dusted and cleaned and straightened some of the notices on the pinboard so that they hung at exactly the right angle, he knew what she was thinking, for he was thinking the same thing himself. *What if my boy's run into trouble out there at the roadhouse?*

Still, there was one basic difference between them. Alice's concern for her son was
turning her into an over-protective mother
hen. In her eyes, Rance was still a boy. She
couldn't, or wouldn't, accept that he was a
man now, with a man's abilities and, more
importantly, a man's responsibilities, whereas
Sam had complete faith in Matt, knew he
could look after himself if he had to. So far,
that was something Rance hadn't been given
the chance to do.

He checked the time. It was a quarter after
seven. Outside full dark had descended, and
Little Cody's streetflares were battling
bravely against the wind-driven snow to stay
alight. He watched the woman as she
brushed a strand of wheat-coloured hair
back behind one ear. Waiting was always
tough. But Alice wasn't making it any easier
for either of them.

'Why don't you come an' sit down,
ma'am?' he asked politely. 'We got our prisoner fed an' bedded down for the night. Let's
talk for a while.'

169

She halted and looked at him. Then her shoulders sagged and she came over and sat across from him with a sheepish, sad little smile. 'I'm sorry if I'm getting on your nerves, Mr Judge,' she apologised. 'I know I can be a torment sometimes, with my fretting.'

He shook his head. 'I sure never had you down as a torment, Mrs Colbert. An' my given name is Sam.'

'Very well. Sam. And you may call me Alice.' She glanced up at the wall clock. 'Still, I can't help wondering what is keeping them.'

'Well, they's no tellin' for sure what time they'll be back … Alice. They's some things you can't run to a timetable, law business bein' one of 'em.' He paused a moment, weighing what was in his mind, then took a chance and voiced it. 'It can be hard, lettin' go. But it's always been my experience that it generally works out for the good o' both parties.'

She looked at him sharply. 'What is that

supposed to mean?'

He shrugged, having a sudden change of heart. 'Aw, nothin'. I'm sorry, I guess it was none of my beeswax. My apologies, ma'am.'

She looked down into her mug, curling both hands around it to warm them through. 'You're saying that I worry *too* much about Rance, aren't you?'

He nodded. 'Yes'm, I guess I am.'

She allowed that a moment to sink in, then accepted it with a jerky little nod. 'I know I can be ... well, too *maternal*, I suppose you could say. I always have been. He was a sickly child, you know. And because his father ... went ... and Rance took over the job of marshal, I've gotten worse, I know I have.' She turned her china-blue eyes directly onto him. 'But is that so bad? Wouldn't the world be a better place if mothers gave their children more love and attention?'

He shifted in the creaking chair as fresh snow tip-tapped at the barred window. 'Love an' attention're all right up to a point, Alice,' he said. 'But sometimes you got to know when to quit.'

'Do you have any children ... Sam?'

He hesitated before saying, 'No.'

'Then I hardly think you are in a position to offer me advice, do you?' she said archly.

He shook his head, not wanting to get into an argument over it. 'No. No, you're right, ma'am. I'm sorry if I spoke out of turn.'

Impulsively Alice got up and began to wander around the room again, shaking her head irritably, all twitchy and fired-up. 'No, I'm *not* right, Sam. I'm wrong. I know it. But...' She paused, looked over at him, then came back and sat down again. 'Haven't I got a right to worry? The Powells are dangerous people.'

He cracked a cool smile. 'I've seen Matt when he's riled,' he replied. 'I tell you, he can be pretty dangerous himself.'

'You think a lot of him, don't you?'

'He's about the best partner I ever had.'

Another blast of icy wind buffeted the building, making the walls creak. Alice shivered and said, 'I'll be glad when winter's behind us.'

'Me too.'

'Is that so you can be moving on again?'

'Uh-huh.'

'It must be a lonely life on the trail, with no real place to call home.'

'It *can* be.'

'I didn't realise how lonely life could be until Vernon ... that's Rance's father ... left us.'

Assuming a look of commiseration, Sam asked, 'Did your man go all of a sudden, ma'am?'

She returned his look blankly for a moment, then confessed, 'He didn't pass on – Sam. He ... left me. A saloon-hall trollop was passing through about eighteen months ago and ... well, he was at the age where the attention of a younger, prettier woman appealed to his vanity. When she left town, he went with her, and at the finish I cannot truly say that I was sorry to see him go.'

Sam struggled to think of something to say to that, then decided that there wasn't a whole lot. In the end his Texas chivalry came back to the fore and he said, 'Well, I'll tell you this much, ma'am. That there saloon-hall trollop must sure have been a looker to've tempted any man away from you.'

She regarded him in some surprise. 'Why, thank you, Sam. That's a very kind thing to say.'

'I mean it, ma'am.'

She did some more of that blushing she'd done earlier, and cast her eyes down to the floor, all demure-like. 'I wonder. Please don't think me forward, but...'

'Yes'm?'

Her eyes came up to him once more. 'Would you care to come to dinner to-morrow evening? You've been such a help to us these past couple of days, it's the least I could do. Young Matt is included in the invitation as well, of course.'

'We'd appreciate that, Alice. A genuine home-cooked meal ... that there is a power-ful temptation to resist. You don't know how sick a man can get of eatin' his own cookin'.

Uh, not that I'd be complainin' about the company, either.'

Her smile was the real thing, and it chased off some of her worry-lines. 'That's settled, then,' she said. 'Shall we say seven o'clock? Rance will give you directions.'

'I look–'

He broke off without warning and came up out of his chair, and Alice put a hand to her mouth and said in alarm, 'What is it, Sam? What's the matter?'

'Riders comin' in,' he said.

Together they went over to the window and looked past their ghostly reflections. Sam sensed the sudden, weakening sense of relief that washed through Alice as they identified the silhouettes of Rance and Matt. 'Oh, thank God they're back safely!'

Outside, the newcomers dismounted stiffly, looped their reins over the hitch-rail out front and came inside, whitened by the squall, stamping snow onto the floor as they entered and batted damp hats against their legs.

Rance and Matt unbuttoned their coats

and flopped into chairs, tired out by the ride. Alice poured them coffee. At last Sam said, 'How'd it go?'

Matt looked at him through rising steam. The exertions of the afternoon had bleached the colour out of him. His dark, curly hair was damp around the edges and he looked weary. 'Lije Tucker ambushed us,' he said. 'I killed him.'

Alice's mouth dropped open. 'Heavens! Are you both all right? Rance, are you—'

'We're fine,' Rance said, trying to mask his irritation at her fussing. 'But I think me and my deputy here better sleep with one eye open till the trial's over.'

'You figure them Powells'll try somethin' else?'

'I'm sure they will, Mr Judge. Moreso now, after what happened to Lije.'

Between them, Rance and Matt gave a fuller account of their ride out to the road-house and the reaction of the Powells to Lije's death. Meanwhile, Alice disappeared into the jailhouse, and returned a moment later with a shaggy-headed mop with which to dry the floor.

Thirty minutes later Sam rose and reached for his hat and coat. 'Well, we might's well all get some rest while we still can, I guess. Sure enough, the next few days're gonna be full, if you fellers're right.' As he shrugged into his jacket and went over to the door, he turned his head to address Alice. 'If that invite still holds…?'

She nodded. 'It does.'

'Look forward to it, then,' he said with a wink.

He and Matt nodded their goodnights and stepped out into the street. Matt untied his horse and then he and Sam started off towards their hotel.

'So,' said Matt, eyeing his companion speculatively. 'What's all this about an invite?'

'Aw, Alice invited us to her place for dinner.'

'"Alice", is it?' Matt stifled a yawn. 'You sure she meant us, and not just you?'

Sam's response was a growl. 'I'm sure.'

'It's just that I'd hate to think you've been making up to that woman while we've been gone. Catching her when she's got her guard down.'

'Son, anyone ever tell you you got a real dirty mind? 'Fact, it was real fine, me an' Alice keepin' each other company while you two dragged your asses back here.'

'Oh, I'll just bet it was fine.'

Sam proffered some advice. 'Best you wash your mouth out afore you say your prayers tonight, Matthew.'

They split up, Matt to lead his pony around to the stable behind the hotel, Sam to go on up to their room. When Matt joined him fifteen minutes later, however, Sam was sitting on the edge of his unmade bed, stroking a frankly sorry-looking Mitzi.

Closing the door behind him, Matt said with a frown, 'What's up?'

Sam shook his head. 'Don't know, I jus' came in an' found her like this, all weak an' lifeless.'

Matt bent to study the cat in the overhead

lamplight. Mitzi blinked back at him from out of vague, glazed eyes. He fingered the fur between her ears and said softly, 'What is it, girl? Eh? What's ailing you?'

Mitzi opened her mouth and managed a miserable little meow, then craned forward to run her sandpapery tongue across his hand.

Matt pointed to the last of the scraps Sam had put down for her that morning. 'Maybe she overloaded her belly.'

'Maybe,' Sam agreed fretfully. 'But she ain't never done that before.' He studied the cat thoughtfully, then sighed. 'Let her rest for tonight, an' we'll see how she is tomorrow. Maybe she's just caught a cold or somethin'.'

On the bed, Mitzi meowed again and closed her eyes. She'd caught a whole sight more than that.

Court convened again at ten o'clock the following morning. The angry thunder of Judge Moffat's gavel fifteen minutes later signalled another adjournment.

Having decided that discretion was the better part of valour, five more jurors had dropped out overnight. One had sent a note to say he was ill. Another had stopped by the marshal's office to say that he had to go visit an elderly, dying relative. The rest just plain hadn't bothered to turn up.

'Very well,' Judge Moffat said, peering around the makeshift courtroom over his cracked spectacles. 'It appears that we have no option but to select a new jury and start from scratch. If you would be so kind as to call twelve new jurors, Marshal Colbert.'

Rance stepped forward and ran his honest blue eyes across the crowd. There was a lot of fidgeting then, and a lot of folks who suddenly found it easier to look at the walls, the ceiling, the hands in their laps, their feet.

'Allen Nordyke,' he called after a moment.

A tall, thin man in a big, unbuttoned jacket tried to pretend that his name wasn't Allen Nordyke at all, until Rance called him again. Then the man rose to his feet and

Rance said, 'Step up here, Allen, and take the oath.'

Allen Nordyke swallowed hard. He thought about it for a moment, then cleared his throat and said, 'No sir.'

There was a sudden outbreak of muttering among the onlookers, and Judge Moffat banged his gavel again and said, 'Silence in court! You, Mr Nordyke. Maybe you didn't understand. This isn't an invitation we're giving here, it's an order! You don't have any choice in the matter!'

Nordyke was sweating despite the seeping chill of the hall. He shifted his weight from one foot to the other as he struggled to get words out past the nervous lump in his throat. Finally he said, 'You think I'm puttin' me or my folks at risk like them other jurors did, you better think again, Your Judgeship.'

Judge Moffat's round, lined face turned livid. 'You've been summoned by this court to serve on the jury, Nordyke. You'll step up here and do exactly that, or I'll hold you in contempt!'

Gaining more confidence because he sensed that he was speaking for everyone, Nordyke said, 'Well, you do that, judge, 'cause I'm sure as heck not servin' on no jury at *this* trial.'

Alvin Clark seized the opportunity to rise to his feet. 'Your Honour,' he said. 'Since the court seems unable to summon a jury, I would like to suggest that you dismiss this case and let everyone go about their business.'

Bob Robbins sprang up at once. 'Objection, Your Honour! That is out of the question!'

'With respect, Your Honour, I must insist,' Clark went on earnestly. 'A woman was killed here in Little Cody, and only the most circumstantial evidence links my client to that murder. But these people have already made up their minds as to his guilt. You cannot guarantee him a fair trial. You can't even get the trial *started!*'

Judge Moffat struggled to remain patient. 'Mr Clark, the reason we can't get the trial started is because of the intimidatory tactics employed by the defendant's family.'

'I must ask you to withdraw that statement, Your Honour! That's only hearsay, and you have no hard evidence to back it up.'

'Facts are facts, Mr Clark. And I speak from first-hand experience, don't forget.'

'Even so, Your Honour, I feel it only right to request a retraction of the slur you cast upon the defendant's family, otherwise I will have to seriously consider levelling a charge of malicious prosecution against you!'

'Mr Clark, I will ask you once more to resume your seat. I know perfectly well that you're trying to blur the issue here, but it won't work. Mr Nordyke, you may leave this hall. But hear this. I find you guilty of contempt of court and hereby fine you fifty dollars, which Marshal Colbert will be around to collect later today. Failure or refusal to pay this fine will result in fourteen days in jail. Do you understand that?'

Nordyke grabbed his hat, glared at the

judge and then stalked out of the hall. With a sigh, the judge said, 'Very well, marshal. Call another juror, if you will.'

Rance did, and they got lucky that time. The towner came up, reluctantly took the oath and went to sit in one of the seats reserved for the jury. But when Rance called the next man up, they once again met with a stubborn refusal to serve, and the same thing happened again when they tried to call the man after that.

In exasperation the judge called for silence. As the edgy townsfolk gradually quietened, the old man scowled at them. Eventually it grew so quiet that you could've heard a snowflake drop.

Finally the judge said, 'After what happened to the other jurors yesterday, I understand the reluctance of you people to get involved in this case. But understanding it is one thing. Excusing it is something else entirely. You people have a moral obligation to see that justice is done here.

'Now, Mr Clark has suggested that I

dismiss this case because we can't get the trial started. Is that what you people want?'

The floor, the walls, the ceiling ... suddenly they all became fascinating things to look at again.

'No, I didn't think so,' Moffat said. 'It strikes me that you might be more willing to cooperate if we could guarantee you some kind of protection. All right. I will see what can be done about that. In the meantime, I'm temporarily suspending this hearing until I've had a chance to consult with Marshal Colbert.'

Townsfolk spilled gratefully out into the street and then dispersed to all points of the compass. Rance unlocked the manacle holding Tom Powell to his chair and told him to get up. Tom obliged slowly, with a contemptuous grin on his pale, sharp-looking face, and submitted meekly while Rance cuffed his hands behind his back.

Holding the key out to Matt, the marshal said, 'Take him back to jail for me, will you? I'll be along in a while.'

With a nod, Matt grabbed Tom by the shoulder of his old check jacket and shoved him toward the doors. Tom went at his own relaxed, leisurely pace, his every move a challenge, a statement of his own imagined supremacy.

Out in the street, they turned down towards the office, walking side by side. Tom grinned at everyone who dared to look up at him as they passed. Either he didn't understand that Judge Moffat really was determined to try him, or he had total confidence in his family to get him off the charge.

As they walked, he glanced speculatively at Matt's profile. At last he said, 'It true, what I heard? That you killed my brother-in-law?'

Drawing in a heavy breath, Matt slanted a brief look at him. As he let it out he said, 'It's true.'

Tom shook his head in disapproval. 'Well, that was a bad thing to do, deputy. For all his faults, I liked ol' Lije.' He looked Matt up and down. 'You never took him from the front, I bet. You couldn't have. Lije was a sharp man with a gun.' He grinned like a wolf. 'You must've back-shot him.'

'I never was much of a one for back-shooting a man,' Matt replied, refusing to be drawn by the insult.

They walked on through the faint morning sunshine. Then Tom asked, 'How'd my sister take it?'

'How do you think? Hard.'

'Don't know why. Weren't no love lost between Evie an' Lije,' Tom responded. 'Still, I can see how she'd take it personal, somethin' like that. Tell you somethin' else, too. If she don't kill you over it, *I* will.'

Matt looked more closely at him. 'You sound awful sure of yourself.'

'Why not? You think these people got balls enough to try me? An' even if they do, you think they'd dare find me guilty?'

'I'm *sure* they will.'

'Uh-huh. I'll walk out of here a free man, just you watch me. Then I'll settle with you for what you done to Lije. An' that'll be a pure pleasure.'

'You hold to that thought, Tom,' Matt told him as they reached the office. 'It might just help keep your mind off what it's gonna be like when they finally get around to hanging you.'

The courthouse emptied out until the only people left were the judge, Rance, Alvin Clark, Bob Robbins, Sam and Alice. As they gathered around the judge's bench, the judge himself said, 'All right. I've told the people we're going to guarantee their safety. Now we have to decide how best we can do just that.'

Alvin Clark pointed to Sam and Alice. 'This is highly irregular, having civilians present while we discuss such matters, judge.'

Bob Robbins said, 'Mr Clark, why don't you just climb down off your high horse for a moment?'

Lew Moffat agreed. 'Mr Judge is here because he has a vast wealth of experience in this and other law-enforcement matters. Mrs Colbert is present because, until the marshal took on his new deputy yesterday, she was as good as a deputy to him herself, and she understands both the nature of the case and the family from whom we are proposing to protect our jurors.'

'You're slandering my client's family again, judge,' began Clark.

'Mr Clark,' said Judge Moffat. 'Button it.' He turned to the rest of the assembly. 'Now – any suggestions?'

Rance spoke up. 'We've got to find twelve men with the least to lose. Bachelors. Widowers. Men whose families can't be intimidated.'

'Can you find twelve such men?'

He thought about it. 'I could probably rustle up half a dozen. Maybe.'

'And the rest?'

'*There* we'd have some problems.'

Judge Moffat scratched his chin. 'Mr Judge? Have you ever come across a situation like this before?'

Sam shook his head. 'Uh-huh. But I'm jus' wonderin'. How long do you suppose it'd take you to present your evidence, Mr Robbins?'

The school superintendent considered. 'As far as I can see, it's an open and shut case. About an hour, hour and a half.'

'An' how long're you proposin' to argue about it, Clark?'

Clark said, 'What kind of question is that?'

'Yes, Sam,' said Alice. 'What *are* you trying to get at?'

'That you can't jus' go ahead an' pick the jury *you* want for the job. That's as good as riggin' it. An' there's no way you can hope to protect every juror an' his family from the Powells, not without a whole squad o' deputies to help you. But if you can guarantee to get the case heard in jus' the one day, it'd be possible to keep an eye on 'em all right *here.*'

Alice frowned. '*What?*'

'With all a man's relations right here in court where he can see 'em, with his wife lookin' after his kids in that room you been usin' out back, judge, an' me or Matt or even Alice here to keep an eye on 'em, all them jurors'd have to worry about is their homes – an' there'd be nothin' to gain by damagin' their property, save retaliation. For the duration of the trial, they'd be practically untouchable.'

Judge Moffat considered it. He took off his spectacles and pinched the flesh at the bridge of his nose. 'Think you can tie all this up in a day, Mr Clark?' he asked.

'I suppose,' Clark answered grudgingly. 'But I'm not happy about it.'

'Then perhaps you should instruct your client's family to stop trying to interfere with due process and allow us to give him a fairer, more unhurried trial?'

Clearly Clark didn't much fancy riding out to the roadhouse to suggest that.

The judge put his glasses back on and looked at Rance. 'Well, marshal? What do you think?'

'I don't reckon we've got any choice in the matter, judge. I'll spread the word that court will reconvene tomorrow morning at, say, nine o'clock. Then – and *only* then – we'll tell the people what we're proposing to do. Once we've chosen a new jury, Mr Judge, my mother, my deputy and me can go round up their families and bring them back here. It's not a perfect plan, but in the circumstances it's about the best I think we're going to get.'

'Very well, marshal, I leave it in your hands.' The judge scanned them all, paying particular attention to Clark. 'And remember – not a word of this to anyone. We don't want to tip our hand.'

The discussion over, the judge got up and hobbled off to collect his things and return to his hotel. Rance nodded his farewells and headed back to his office. As Clark and Robbins gathered their papers together, Sam asked Alice if he might escort her back to her house and she said, why thank you kindly.

As they stepped out onto the street Sam held out his arm. 'Best you hang onto me, Alice,' he said. 'Some of this ice is fair treacherous.'

She took his arm and the slight pressure of her tiny hand felt good.

'Anyway,' she said. 'Before the judge called the court to order, you were telling me about your cat.'

'Oh yeah,' he nodded. 'Not that there's all that much to tell. I found her lookin' like death warmed over las' night, but this mornin' she was pretty much back to her ol' self, couldn't hardly wait to go out for a stroll aroun' town. I guess she must've picked up a bug or somethin'.'

As they worked higher up the slope towards the cabins that dotted the grade to the south of town, Alice said without preamble, 'You were right, you know. It *is* hard to let go.'

He frowned. 'Ma'am?'

She kept looking straight ahead. 'I thought about what you were saying last night. I thought about it a lot. You were right, Sam. There comes a time when you *have* to let go, even if you don't want to. But that's what life is all about, isn't it? First of all you have to let go of your childhood, then your adolescence, your parents, your innocence, your own children ... and finally, your life.'

'That's a pretty deep way o' puttin' it,' he said. 'But I think I can see what you're sayin'.'

They reached the summit, both breathing hard into the frosty air. Sam turned around to look back down at the town. It looked like a painting at this elevation, roofs swollen to twice their normal size with snow, smoke tufting out of chimneys to ride the fitful breeze, beetle-sized horses pulling creaking wagons along the main stem, and people scurrying around them like busy ants.

Twenty yards further on, they came to a small, spotless cabin with real glass windows, and Alice said, 'Would you care to come in for a cup of coffee now that you're here, Sam?'

Sam beamed a winning smile at her. 'Why, that'd be swell, Alice.'

As the day wore on, the clouds thinned and the sun broke through. Although the temperature refused to lift much above freezing, even the briefest glimpse of the blue sky and good, strong daylight was sufficient to raise the spirits.

One cup of coffee turned into three, plus a handsome wedge of home-baked seed cake, and it was sometime after noon when Sam left Alice's place with a promise to come back at seven. By then the daylight was fading and more clouds were pushing back in from the north.

Hands shoved into his pockets, Sam retraced his steps down into town. Finding Mitzi slinking around the hotel reception (much to the disapproval of the clerk behind the desk), he picked her up and took her down to Rance's office, stopping off at the meat market once again to pick up some more scraps for her. On the surface, the fat cat seemed to be back to her old self, and yet Sam could tell that there was something about her that still wasn't quite *right*.

He entered the office to find Matt and Rance just finishing off a meal they'd had sent over from the restaurant across the street. Setting Mitzi down in the corner and opening up the paper in which the scraps had been wrapped, he then came over to join them.

As he pulled up a chair, Matt offered him a look of mock regret. 'Got some bad news for you, Sam,' he said. 'Rance's got a feeling that the Powells'll have another go at Judge Moffat if they can't get at the jury. Wants me to keep an eye on him tonight.'

'That mean you can't make it to Mrs Colbert's for supper?'

''Fraid so.'

'That's too bad,' Sam said, not meaning a syllable of it. 'But it can't be helped, I guess. I'll give her your apologies.'

Rance got up and stretched his back, then wandered across the room to crouch and stroke Mitzi as she made little *crunch-crunch-crunch* sounds over the pile of scraps. 'Do you think this idea of yours can really work, Mr Judge?' he asked.

Sam produced a cigar and a match. 'It's

like you said earlier, Rance. We ain't got no choice.'

'But what about afterwards? What if the Powells try to single out the jurors once the trial's over?'

He'd straightened up and glanced out the window. He always liked to keep an eye on Main, but more so just lately. Now, as Sam made to form a reply to him, he saw the marshal's shoulders square a little and frowned at him. 'Somethin' wrong, son?'

Rance looked at him. 'I don't know.'

Picking up something in his tone, Sam and Matt rose and crossed the office to join him. Four riders were just reining down in front of Brady's Saloon, big, dusty-looking men, all heavily garbed against the cold. As they dismounted, the dying sunshine caught on the sharp rowels of their spurs. They tied up at the rack and pushed into the saloon, but not before one of them held back and glanced around at their new surroundings.

He was long and lean, with a thick gunbelt buckled over an old plaid jacket and patched, cavalry-issue pants tucked into worn black boots. He had a strong, quite handsome face beneath the brim of his distinctive Jeff Davis campaign hat, with dark eyes, a straight nose and a big handlebar moustache obscuring a bleak mouth.

Matt said, 'You know 'em, Rance?'

Rance nodded. 'I know that big feller in the Jeff Davis,' he replied. 'And having him in *this* town at *this* time makes me feel real uneasy.'

Sam eyed him impatiently. 'You gonna tell us who he is, or you gonna keep us in suspense?' he asked.

Rance turned away from the window and reached his hat and coat down off the wall-pegs. 'It's Dan Wheelahan,' he said grimly. 'Tom Powell's cousin.'

SEVEN

As Rance pulled on his jacket he said, 'Wheelahan runs a horse ranch up along the Tongue, nothing big, just a couple of sheds and corrals. Up till about two years ago he was in the army. Now he supplies remounts to Fort Custer – when he's not lifting other men's stock and generally raising Cain, that is. We don't usually see him in this neck of the woods – which makes me twice as wary of seeing him here now.'

As he planted his hat firmly on his head and strode to the door, Sam said, 'Mind if I tag along, son?'

Rance turned on him and said sharply, 'I can handle this just fine on my own, Mr Judge.'

'Never said otherwise,' Sam replied without offence. 'But they's four o' them, an' only one o' you. Seems to me it'd make good sense to cut down them odds.'

Rance searched his face for a moment, then relaxed. 'Tell me something, Mr Judge,' he said. 'Has Matt ever told you you've got an irritating habit of always being right?' Cracking a smile he said, 'Come ahead and welcome. Truth to tell, I'd appreciate the company.'

Leaving Matt to watch the prisoner, they quit the office, crossed the street and went into the saloon. A few late-afternoon drinkers had been conversing up at the bar, but with the arrival of Wheelahan and his companions, several of them had been overcome with another attack of nerves and were just leaving.

Wheelahan and the others were sharing a bottle and coffee over at a round, baize-topped table at the rear of the long, over-heated room. Rance spotted them as soon as his eyes adjusted to the dim, smoky light and he approached them at a slow, cautious walk, his boots drumming a soft tattoo against the sawdusted boards.

Wheelahan glanced up and watched him come, Sam right behind him. The former soldier was in his early thirties, and wore his dark, curly brown hair to well below the nape of his neck. He reached his right hand across the table and tilted the bottle to his mug. When he spoke, his voice was deep and assured.

'Hello there, Colbert. Buy you a drink?'

Rance shook his head. 'No thanks. I just came to find out what brings *you* to town.'

Wheelahan smiled. He had faintly yellow teeth. He said, 'Why, I should've thought that was obvious. You're tryin' my cousin for murder, ain't you? I come to make sure he gets a fair crack o' the whip.'

'And that brought you sixty-odd miles, in *this* weather?'

'Sure.' Wheelahan squinted at him. 'Whatsa matter, Colbert? Ain't you never heard of a family that sticks together?'

It was an obvious reference to Rance's absent father, and realising that, the towners

201

still standing up at the bar froze in horrified silence, their worried eyes fixed on their marshal, wondering how he was going to react to it.

Rance stiffened dangerously for a moment. The words had caught him more like a slap. Sam wanted to tell him to keep a cool head, that Wheelahan was only trying to goad him, but held his peace, knowing better than to butt in.

After another moment, Rance forced an easy smile onto his face. 'What does that make these fellers, then?' he asked, indicating the horse-rancher's trio of companions. 'Your legal advisers?'

Wheelahan chuckled this time. 'Naw, naw, nothin' like that. They work for me.'

'They got names?'

'Uh-huh.'

'Well, I'd appreciate to hear 'em.'

Wheelahan worked clockwise around the table. The man to his left was Emmett Carson. Carson was a tall, bony man in his late twenties, dressed in corduroy breeches and a sheepskin jacket. He looked up and nodded a brusque howdy. One of his muddy brown eyes was off-centre and he had a straggly excuse for a beard lining his chin.

Next to him sat a shorter, squatter, older man with a thicker black beard and very small, very deep-set, very dark eyes whose name was Frank Wilson. He was tending towards the gut and had the look of a man who liked his drink. He never even glanced up when Wheelahan spoke his name.

The last man wasn't even out of his teens yet. He was clean-shaven, expressionless, and he had the dusky complexion of a halfbreed – part Blackfoot, Sam thought, judging by the single eagle feather that adorned his fur hat, and the unusual hooded blanket coat he favoured. His name, Wheelahan said, was Denver Tree.

'Right,' nodded Rance. 'Listen up, all of you. I'm putting you on notice. First sign I get that you boys're here to make trouble, you'll be keeping Cousin Tom company in jail. Understand that, Dan?'

Wheelahan's face sobered and suddenly he looked older, uglier, more dangerous. 'You got no call to threaten us, Colbert. We only just got here.'

'That's as maybe. But I know your reputation, Dan. You're a firebrand from way back, and your men here look like they're cut from the same cloth. I don't intend to take a chance on any of you.'

Wheelahan's grin returned. 'Now don't go scarin' me, marshal,' he said. 'I only got the one pair o' clean drawers.'

He diluted his coffee with another splash of whiskey as his friends did some sniggering at his coarse attempt at humour. At length he spoke again. 'Be all right if I visit with Cousin Tom later on?'

'I guess.'

The horse-rancher lifted his spiked mug in toast. 'Well, I guess that's about it, then. You came over here for some answers. Now you've got 'em, you can move along. Me an' my partners here been on the trail a long time. We want to get a little merry an' then find us a bite to eat an' a bed for the night.'

Rance nodded. 'All right, Dan. Just so long as you keep it down.'

He turned away and together he and Sam got halfway to the door before Wheelahan called after them. 'I see your mama still ain't lettin' you out on your own, Rance.'

Rance spun on him.

The horse-rancher reached up to wipe at his damp moustache. 'I mean, your buddy there's too damn' old to be a deputy, so I figure he's just got to be your nursemaid,' he remarked mordantly.

Emmett Carson chuckled. Frank Wilson snorted. Denver Tree just stared into his mug.

For his part, Rance gave no immediate reaction. Then he went slowly back across to the table, and Sam felt the rage coming off him in waves. Trouble was coming so fast that there was nothing anyone there could do to avert it – indeed, Sam couldn't help thinking that any attempt *to* avert it would only hasten its arrival.

Rance stopped then, and leaned down over the table with his palms flat against the baize top. He looked straight into Wheelahan's eyes and held them, and not for the first time Sam felt a sneaking admiration for him.

'I'll tell you something about that "old" man,' Rance said softly. 'That's Sam Judge, Dan. That's right – Sam Judge. And since Sam was arresting better men than you when you were still just a promise in your old man's pants, I'd advise strongly against riling him.'

Emmett Carson chuckled again, then fell quiet. Once more Wheelahan's face went dead and dangerous, but Rance kept on staring at him until finally Wheelahan had to sit back in order to put a little distance between them.

Rance pushed away from the table a moment later, then turned without another word and resumed his journey to the door. Sam fell in beside him and together they pushed back out into the coming dusk, feeling the horse-rancher's eyes burning into them until the door swung shut again and they were finally out of sight.

Night draped a dark blanket across the town, and the temperature plunged to ten below. Up at their hotel room, Sam finished shaving, rinsed the last of the soap from his long, weathered face, then dried himself off and studied his reflection critically in the old, out-of-place triple-mirror dressing-table.

Finally satisfied that he would pass muster, he reached for his spare shirt and finished dressing.

It was as he was shrugging into his vest that he noticed Mitzi curling sluggishly into a ball on his bed, and as he went over to her he had a nasty feeling that whatever had been plaguing her the previous evening was back again tonight.

She looked up at him and meowed wretchedly. He picked her up and was startled by just how distended her stomach felt. Raising her up so that he could inspect her closer in the lamplight, he saw that her belly looked blotchy and tight.

'What is it, girl? Eh?' he muttered.

Again Mitzi said, *'Meow.'*

Sam put the cat back on the bed and rubbed his smooth jaw. He told himself that she obviously hadn't yet managed to shake off that bug she'd caught. But at the same time he couldn't help thinking, *What if it's something more serious?*

He buckled on his gunbelt and told himself not to be such an old woman. All right, so the cat was poorly. That was all. And even if it turned out to be something fatal, well, it wasn't as if she was human. She was only a cat, after all.

But he knew in his heart that she was much more than that. She was one of the few really long-time companions he'd ever had. And though he would never confess it to another living soul, not even Matt, he had also come to look upon her as a lucky charm.

Aw, he thought with some disgust. *You're a*

sentimental old bastard on the quiet, Sam Judge.

He put on his jacket, clapped down his hat and headed for the door, where he paused for a moment. On impulse, he decided to take the sickly cat with him to Alice's, and tucked her gently under his left arm before buttoning his jacket to the throat.

Outside, Main was still brisk with traffic, and lights showed at the windows of stores and eateries, none of which closed much before nine o'clock, and also the saloons, which usually kept going till around eleven.

Sam scanned the street once: then, just as he was about to start off, he saw the door to the marshal's office swing open and Dan Wheelahan step out into the street.

That in itself was no surprise, of course. Wheelahan had mentioned wanting to visit with his cousin earlier on. But as the horse-rancher crossed the street in a string of long, determined strides, Sam decided to follow another impulse – this one, to follow him.

He allowed Wheelahan to get some distance ahead and then dogged him along the line of mis-matched buildings until he came to Brady's Saloon. There he swung right, pushed into the place and let the door slam shut behind him.

Brady's Saloon.

Well, that was no surprise either, he guessed.

Sam halted outside the place. Lamplight shimmered out across his face from a nearby window, and the miniaturised reflection of the window itself showed in his mild grey eyes.

He moved closer to the window and peered inside.

Wheelahan was a big man and he dominated the room. He made directly for the table at which Rance had braced him earlier. He sat down, put his elbows on the baize top and started talking while one of his men poured him a drink and nudged the glass towards him.

Sam looked at them. Dan Wheelahan. Emmett Carson. Frank Wilson. Denver Tree.

And *Alvin Clark.*

Sam wasn't sure what he should read into Clark's presence. Maybe nothing. Wheelahan was kin to the Powells, after all. Perhaps Clark was there to give him a professional opinion on how he expected the trial to go.

Still…

Sam felt uneasy. There was something about Clark that was hard to like, and something else that was even harder to trust.

Beneath his arm, Mitzi shifted restlessly, and Sam's thoughts returned to the sick animal. 'Easy, girl,' he murmured, giving the cat a gentle squeeze through the material of his jacket.

He turned away from the saloon and set off back the way he'd just come, head dipped against the freshening wind, until eventually he found himself climbing the slope that led up to Alice's house, and the town lights were just a cluster of fireflies in the distance below.

He went up to her door, cleared his throat, brushed himself down one final time, then knocked. She answered the door almost at once, and the cosy glow of the lamplit parlour behind her threw a golden halo around her as she smiled at him.

'Sam,' she said, as if she'd expected someone else. 'Come in.'

He did. The house was neat, tidy and homely. A fire crackled in the hearth, and the thick curtains had been pulled against the frosty darkness. The heavy oak dining table had been set for three people, he noticed.

'Where's Matt?' she asked.

'He couldn't make it,' Sam replied. 'Rance's got him ridin' shotgun on Judge Moffat. But he sends his apologies.'

'That's a shame. Is Rance expecting trouble, then?'

'I suspicion he jus' wants to be prepared.'

Walking past her into the parlour, he unbuttoned his jacket and she came up behind him, took hold of the shoulders and helped him out of it. 'Then it's just you and me,' she said, keeping her voice neutral.

'Not quite, Alice,' he replied, turning

around so that she could see the cat he was cradling. 'You bein' such a fine, upstandin' lady an' all … well, I thought it'd be best iffen I fetched a chaperone.'

Alice smiled up at him. She seemed almost relieved to have some third party there, even if it was just a fat, frowsy cat.

'She's ill again, Alice,' Sam said gravely.

Alice regarded the feline. 'Settle her down by the fire,' she said. 'I'll fetch her a bowl of water, and then see how supper's doing.'

Matt and Judge Moffat ate a late supper in the restaurant of Little Cody's finest hotel, the Hardin House, where the judge was also staying.

Much of the earlier part of the evening had been spent down at Rance's office, discussing their present difficulties, and the means by which they hoped to complete the trial the following day, although there had been a temporary lull at around a quarter of six, when Dan Wheelahan came in and said he was there to visit with Cousin Tom.

Rance told him to surrender his weapons before he went through, and Wheelahan had unbuckled his gunbelt, coiled it around the converted Navy Colt in the pocket and handed it over, smirking all the while beneath his thick, dark moustache.

Rance had put the gunbelt on his desk, checked Wheelahan himself for any other weapons, and discovered a skinning knife hidden in a pocket of the man's right boot and a Remington double derringer stuffed into his pants'-belt at the small of his back.

Finally he escorted the horse-rancher into the cell-block and came back a short time later.

Wheelahan's visit lasted about twenty minutes. When he came back out into the office and retrieved his weapons, he said very little but smirked a whole lot. Before he left, however, he fixed Judge Moffat with a curious stare, then said, 'You just gotta be that judge I been hearin' about.'

The judge puffed up his chest defiantly. 'I am Lew Moffat, yes,' he replied.

Wheelahan indicated the judge's cane. 'They tell me you pack a fair clout with that thing, judge.'

'Oh? And ... and who are "they"?'

Wheelahan's shrug was elaborate. 'Oh, just folks.' He smiled at them, although there was no warmth in the sudden flash of his yellowing teeth. 'Well, be seein' you.'

The door clicked shut behind him.

Up till then, Judge Moffat had felt that Rance was being over-cautious in giving him a bodyguard, but now he wasn't so sure. 'I've heard of this Wheelahan before,' he mused. 'And a thoroughly unpleasant piece of work he seems to be, too. I had no idea that he and the Powells were related.'

'Oh, they're related, all right,' Rance responded grimly. He moved over to the window and watched Wheelahan dodge traffic to get across the road. 'I've got a bad feeling about that man,' he muttered.

'Me too,' Matt agreed. 'I almost hate to say it, but I've got the feeling he's been drafted in.'

The judge frowned. '*What?*'

'I think Nathan Powell sent Saul to fetch him and his men here to help intimidate you and whoever serves on tomorrow's jury, judge. That's why Saul wasn't out at the roadhouse yesterday afternoon.'

'And *that,*' said Rance, 'is why I want Matt here to keep an eye on you this evening.'

Lew Moffat rose to his feet, pushing himself erect with the help of his stick. 'I appreciate your kindness, Marshal Colbert,' he said. He turned his spectacles onto Matt. 'Well, since we are to be companions, young man, perhaps you will allow me to buy you supper?'

Matt grinned and reached for his hat. 'Oh, I think I could be persuaded.'

The food at the Hardin Hotel was good and the conversation was interesting. But Judge Moffat tired easily, and by the time they were ready to finish off their meal with a fresh pot of coffee, the old man's eyelids were drooping.

Finally they rose and strolled out into the

lobby and said their goodnights at the foot of the wide staircase.

'You be all right now, judge?'

Moffat smiled. 'Quite all right, thank you – although you're welcome to come up and check under my bed, if it will set your mind at rest.'

'I don't think we'll have to go to those extremes,' Matt replied.

'Well, thank you for a very pleasant evening, Mr Dury.' The judge extended his right hand, his face sober in the guttering lamp-glow. 'I can't tell you how much I have appreciated your company tonight. I am a widower, and I seldom get to see my daughter and her family – they live in Minnesota, you see.'

'Pleasure's been all mine, judge. Goodnight.'

Matt left the hotel and walked back down to the office. It was about a quarter to ten and the odd flake of snow was just starting to spiral to earth.

In the office, Rance was sitting back with

his feet up on his desk, reading an old copy of *The Wide Awake Library*. The moment he heard the door handle begin to turn, he cast the dime novel aside and snatched his gun up off the blotter, then relaxed when he recognised Matt.

'Jumpy?' Matt asked as he came in and shut the winter out.

Rance scowled. 'Uh-huh.'

Want me to spell you for a while?'

'No. I'll bolt the door in a minute and get some sleep. The judge all right?'

'Fine.'

'Well, you might as well get along yourself then.'

'You sure?'

'I'm sure. See you in the morning.'

'All right. I'll take one last stroll around town, then turn in.'

'Thanks.'

Matt paused outside, listening to the sounds Rance made locking up behind him. The town was largely in darkness now, but for the streetflares and what light filtered out through the smudged windows of the saloons. He walked the length of the street, then swung north and back along Cheyenne Road, which ran parallel to Main. Finally his footsteps fetched him back to his hotel and he closed the door behind him with one hand covering a yawn. The lobby was deserted, so he just reached across the desk and took his room-key off the hook, then went upstairs.

He unlocked the door and let himself into the darkness, thinking about tomorrow, wondering how the trial would–

It came to him in that moment that someone else was already in the room, waiting for him, and as a figure came up out of nowhere and slammed into him, he went down with a startled curse.

His blood ran cold then – because the faint glimmer of light coming in through the window flared off a wicked-looking knife – a knife that was plunging towards him in a vicious, killing blur.

As the ornate clock on the mantelpiece finished chiming ten, Sam stirred himself and said, 'Well, it's been a real pleasure, Alice, an' truth to tell, I could go on jus' takin' my ease like this all night … but maybe I ought to be makin' a move.'

Alice had been sitting in an overstuffed chair on the other side of the fire, and now she looked a little sad that their evening together was coming to an end. Still, she covered it well.

'It's me who should be thanking you,' she said, sitting forward. 'You don't know what a change it's been, having you here this evening.'

Sam gestured to Mitzi, who was all but lost in the folds of an old blanket beside the fire. 'An' you're *sure* you don't mind lookin' after Mitzi for me?'

'Not at all.'

'Well, I'd sure feel happier, knowin' someone was with her all the time, 'cause I'm pure stumped as to what might be ailin' her.'

They rose and Alice bustled out of the room to fetch his jacket, leaving Sam himself to study the framed dagguereotypes that littered the mantel.

He smiled down at Alice's very prim, starched, much younger likeness, telling himself that she had always been a handsome woman, even back then, when she wasn't much past her maturity. His eyes skimmed over a few photographs of Rance, one as a baby, one as a little boy, one as a youth.

Finally he picked up the frame that held a likeness of Vernon Colbert. He appeared to have been a big man, very stern-looking, with oiled hair, a centre parting and a peculiar, oblong-shaped moustache, like the false moustaches they sometimes wore on the stage.

'Looking at my dear departed husband, I see,' Alice said behind him.

He put the frame back on the mantel and turned to face her. She was holding out his coat. He went over and allowed her to help him put it on. They were standing very close together now, a fact which made him feel vaguely ill at ease, but about which he would never dream of complaining.

'I'm a wanderin' man, myself,' he said. 'The one time I set down roots, it darn' near killed me. But if a man had all of this…' His gesture took in the photos and the room.

'Sometimes people just get…' She searched for the right word and finally settled on, '…*tired.*'

He looked down at her, wanting to kiss her very much. But there were some things a man just didn't do, not on such short acquaintance, anyway. So he just brushed past her, grabbed his hat, nodded a farewell to Mitzi and then headed for the door.

The hallway was short and unlit. When he reached the door he turned and said, 'Well. Big day tomorrow.'

She nodded. 'I won't be sorry to see the back of this business. Then perhaps things can start to get back to normal around here.'

He opened the door and said, 'Let's hope. Well … I thank you once again, Alice. It's been dandy, it really has.'

She cast her eyes downward. 'Maybe... Perhaps you'd like to come back and do it all over again before spring thaw comes,' she said.

'Aw, I wouldn't want to impose...'

'It wouldn't be any imposition, Sam, I assure you. In fact I ... I'd like it very much.'

He smiled at her. 'Well, maybe we will, then.'

The night was still. Overhead, clouds were playing tag with each other. He turned his hat in his hands for a moment, not sure how to say goodnight. Eventually, and some might say unimaginatively, he just said, 'Goodnight, then,' and hoped that would suffice.

Not quite masking her disappointment this time, Alice said, 'Goodnight, Sam. I'll see you tomorrow.'

'Uh-huh.'

He backed up a couple of steps, then turned and started down the path and back towards the town, unable to shake the feeling that he'd let her down in some way.

He took four steps, then muttered, 'Aw, hell,' and turned around.

She was framed in the doorway, watching him go. Now she watched him come back, striding towards her like a man with a purpose.

When he finally got back to her he reached out and drew her to him and she tilted her face back to meet his and they kissed, tentatively at first, then with more courage, until suddenly the kiss became a thing of wild passion and need that surprised the pair of them.

At last they broke apart and spent a moment or two just getting their breath back, each studiously avoiding the other's eyes.

'I, ah…' Sam reached up and pawed guiltily at his mouth. 'Maybe I should apologise for that.'

He sensed her gentle smile in the darkness. 'There's no need,' she said.

'But… I mean, I wouldn't want you to run away with any notions that…'

'I won't.'

'I'd hate to hurt you like your husband did, Alice, but I'm a footloose man an' I couldn't make no commitment…'

'Sam,' she said more firmly. 'I understand.'

He felt certain that she did, too.

'Well,' he said. 'I better be goin' an' mean it, this time.'

She nodded. 'Maybe you'd better had. But…'

'Yes'm?'

'Come back tomorrow night, Sam. I'll cook for us again, only this time … this time we'll be celebrating the end of the trial.'

'Alice,' he said seriously as he started backing away again, 'I'm lookin' forward to it already, believe me.'

Matt rolled across the floor, his movements awkward and restricted by his many layers of clothing, and heard the knife thud into the floorboards where he'd just been. He came up in the darkness, breathing hard, heard his opponent's breathing also.

Then the figure straightened up, knife still

in hand, and threw itself at him again, and this time he grabbed the wrist of the hand wielding the knife and squeezed hard until he felt the bones grating together.

His would-be assassin gasped at the pain and swore violently. Matt was in no way startled to recognise Eve Tucker's voice.

With her free hand she tried to claw at his eyes. He swatted her away and squeezed her thin, trapped wrist some more, and finally she had no choice but to release her grip on the knife.

Matt heard it thump against the floor and, still trying to avoid the sharp-nailed talons reaching for his eyes, he booted it out of reach under the bed.

'You ... *bastard!*' she breathed into his face.

He already knew she was beautiful. When he smelled the verbena scent in her hair he realised that she smelled as good as she looked. But she was deadly, too – and the deadliness far outweighed the beauty.

Suddenly she switched tactics and tried to knee him in the crotch. Her knee grazed along his outer thigh instead, and he thrust her away from him roughly, so that she went skittering backwards and connected with the dresser.

In the darkness he saw the triple mirror shudder, heard her groan, saw her silhouette bounce off the dressing table and stagger. The china pitcher and basin tinkled together like a broken music box.

As near as he could tell, she had dressed for warmth like a boy, in a hefty jacket, shirt, pants and heavy boots. He went over to her fast, grabbed her by one arm, yanked her to her feet and said, 'You crazy hellcat! What the *hell* do you think you're playing at?'

That was a dumb question, because the answer was obvious. She stopped struggling in his arms and went limp, so that he was the only thing stopping her from collapsing to the floor, but that was an old trick, and he was too wise a hound to fall for it.

'You can forget all about playin' possum,' he told her harshly. 'You don't strike me as the swooning type, Mrs Tucker.'

She came back to life and started struggling again, and because fighting women was new and frankly unpleasant to him, he thrust her away from him again, so that she staggered back across the room and fell onto Sam's bed.

'Now just hold still!' he ordered.

Through the darkness he heard the bedsprings squeaking as her body weight settled on the mattress.

'*I'll kill you!*' she said.

'Maybe you will,' he replied, calmer now. 'But not tonight you won't.'

'*I hate you!*'

She started crying.

He looked down at her, his breathing slowly regulating. She didn't strike him as being the crying type any more than she'd struck him as being the swooning type. And sure enough, when it became obvious that she wasn't going to earn any sympathy with that, she stopped quite abruptly and looked up at him through the grey darkness.

'I … I don't really hate you,' she said in a

quavery voice that seemed old and drained. 'I … I don't know *how* I feel.'

'*That*,' he said, 'I can believe.'

She ignored the sarcasm and went on. 'Lije wasn't much good, to me *or* himself. But he was the only husband I had, an' you killed him.'

'It was kill or *be* killed, ma'am,' he said. 'You know that.'

She nodded so forcefully that the springs went *squeak-squeak-squeak* again. 'I know. But you got to understand about us Powells. We're a close family, mister, an' we're frightened. Frightened for what these people're gonna do to our Tom.' She shuffled her shapely bottom closer to the edge of the bed and brushed her red hair back off her face. 'If we thought there was one chance in a thousand that Tom'd get a fair trial in Little Cody…'

He snorted tiredly. 'If you want justice, you've got a funny way of going about it.'

'You're just like all the others,' she said petulantly.

'I never said I was anything else.'

'I don't even know your name.'

He stooped to pick up his fallen hat. 'Maybe that's just as well.'

She got up slowly. 'I'm all mixed up,' she said. 'I don't know if I should be tryin' to kill you or ... or tryin' to thank you.'

'Thank me?' He was surprised. 'For killing your man?'

'I told you Lije wasn't up to much. He used to beat me, you know.'

'From what I've seen of you tonight, Mrs Tucker,' Matt said with feeling, 'I don't blame him.'

She came a bit closer, and her voice turned husky. 'I'm cold,' she said, and she sounded it, too. She extended her arms and asked piteously, 'Hold me?'

His expression was one of disgust. 'You can just keep your distance.'

She did. 'What are you gonna do with me, then?'

'I think you'd better join your brother behind bars for a couple of days, till you cool off.'

'*Bastard!*' she spat.

Ah, he thought. *That's more like it.*

He went over to the door and said, 'Come on. Let's go.'

She knuckled her eyes, making one final attempt to appeal to his paternal instincts, then came meekly towards him, stumbling once over the square of rucked-up carpet in the centre of the floor.

She made it look so natural that he didn't think to question it until it was too late. By then, she'd come close to the dresser again, close enough to reach out and sweep the pitcher and basin off the top and straight at him.

The chinaware caught him on one up-raised arm, and the icy contents of both receptacles splashed over him and stole his breath.

Even as they smashed at his feet, Eve was surging past him and out into the hallway.

He roared something incoherent and, dripping cold water off him in a silvery spray, made to tear after her but slipped on a few shards of broken china and lost valuable seconds.

Out in the hallway, Eve made a desperate rush for the stairs and fairly threw herself down them with her luxuriant red hair flying around her face and the frenzy of an about-to-be-caged animal clear in her scheming green eyes.

She heard a sound behind her and chanced a look over one pretty shoulder, expecting to see the young man she'd been hoping to re-christen 'the victim', but he still hadn't shown.

She faced front again and gave an involuntary cry of surprise, because a tall, lean-looking man with a long, vaguely sombre face and a big, round-crowned Stetson had just entered the lobby and was even now climbing the stairs directly in her path.

She saw her own startled surprise mirrored in his face. Then she brought her left arm up and barged roughly past him, leaping the last couple of stairs to the floor.

The man said, *'Hey!'*

Up above, Matt appeared and yelled, *'Get her, Sam!'*

The man, Sam, turned and came after her. She felt his hand grab hold of her sleeve. She came up sharp, spun around, snarled and tried to kick him in the soft parts. The man called Sam danced around that and said sternly, 'Hey now–'

She tried to kick him again, missed again. She saw Sam ball his right hand into a fist and screamed defiantly. 'All right, you sonofabitch – *do your worst!'*

He did.

He clipped her on the jaw and she went, 'Uhn...' and fell down, unconscious.

Standing over her, Sam shook his head. He had no time for men who beat up on women. In his book, they were one of the lowest forms of scum. But there was another rule by which he lived. You never hit a woman unless she had it coming.

Looked like this one had it coming.

Matt came downstairs and into the lobby.

By then most of the other boarders had come awake and were starting to crowd onto the hallways and staircase in order to see what was going on.

'Don't tell me,' said Sam. 'Eve Tucker.'

Matt nodded. But before he could speak, they all heard someone yelling out in the street.

'Fire! Fire!'

The Texans looked at each other.

Outside, the townsman yelled, *'Quick! The municipal hall's alight!'*

EIGHT

Stepping over the prone Eve Tucker, the Texans rushed out into the street. Other people were following their example along the entire length of Main, some of them still tugging on jackets or hats or boots, all of them drawn by the yelling townsman.

They stopped in the middle of the roadway, eyes narrowed against the push of the wind. The sky up at the far end of town held a faint amber brightness, and just behind the municipal hall they saw pointed yellow flames rising steadily higher as the blaze climbed across the back of the frame building and then made a smouldering start on the roof.

Sam watched pungent black smoke stain the red bellies of the clouds racing past overhead. His expression hardened and he muttered, *'Sonsabitches!'*

Then the spell broke. Some of the locals started racing up towards the hall and Sam and Matt immediately fell in beside them. Noise was everywhere – in the frantic bellowing of the men, in the higher, worried entreaties of the women who were telling them to be careful, in the neigh and nicker of confused team and saddle-horses and the excited yapping of nearby dogs.

A bucket brigade had to be organised at once, Sam thought, because even though the fire looked to have consumed much of the back of the meeting place, there was still a chance to limit the damage if only they could act swiftly enough.

But their attempts to get closer and do some good were slowed by the crowd that had gathered solely to watch, and they had to fight their way through that little obstacle before they could scramble and slide madly around the side of the building and see what could be done to extinguish the blaze at the back.

A few rubber-neckers had also ventured

this close, and their milling and shouting was only confusing the matter more. The heat and light were tremendous, the roar and crack of the greedy flames almost enough to burst the eardrums.

There were a whole pack of chiefs around here, and precious few Indians. Sam swore fervently at their lack of initiative. Someone needed to take charge, and quick.

Just then he sensed a commotion in the crowd behind him, and he and Matt turned just as Rance shouldered into sight and started jabbing a finger at various men.

'You, there! I want a bucket brigade organised right away! See to it! You! Hackett, isn't it? Get some men and shovels and try to smother what flames you can with snow! Rest of you, dampen down the surrounding timbers – quick now!'

Once he was through, the young marshal came over to join them, his face stained crimson by the licking, spitting flames, his expression a union of anger, despair and frustration.

'*Dammit!*' he whispered.

Now that something was finally starting to happen to combat the inferno, Sam thought to test the air and found the acrid, unmistakable stench of kerosene on the wind. It was confirmation that the blaze had been started deliberately – not that confirmation was really needed.

'This is Wheelahan's doing, nothing surer!' Rance spat with a curse. 'And damn me if I don't see that he pays for it! I–' He broke off suddenly to start pointing again. 'You men! Don't just stand there, lend a hand!'

Matt cut in. 'Hold up a minute, Rance,' he said. 'Who's minding the store while you're up here?'

Rance looked at him blankly. Clearly he didn't immediately comprehend the implication behind the question. Then, as understanding dawned, a look of unease and apprehension took hold of his face and he looked at the fire again, no longer seeing it as just one more attempt to delay or wreck

Tom Powell's trial, but as a deliberate ploy to get him out of his office and leave Tom all on his own…

He opened his mouth to speak, but Sam got there first. 'Leave it to us, Rance – you've got your hands full here!'

He and Matt pushed back through the crowd and out onto Main, skidding and sliding in the slush. A few wagons, the last of the day's traffic, had stalled along the centre of the street and they had to dodge around horse and vehicle alike as they raced pell-mell down the gentle slope along which Little Cody had grown up.

The wind increased, whipping the street-flares this way and that so that it became difficult to separate a moving shadow from a moving man. Up ahead, the Texans saw a strip of lamplight measuring its length on the planking outside the office. Someone had left the door ajar, and it sure wasn't Rance.

A bunch of saddled horses were hitched to the rack out front, and one man was sitting astride the nearest animal, keeping a look-out, a short, squat man with a generous black beard.

Frank Wilson.

Wilson saw them coming and roared some kind of warning into the cold, dark night. Shadows capered across the floor and wall of what could be seen of the office – men disturbed from their course of action and coming to do something about the intrusion.

All at once the door opened wider and three men burst out with sixguns bucking and blazing – Wheelahan and the rest of his no-good crew.

Sam dodged one way. Matt dodged the other. There was no time to question the situation, only react to it. And since Sam had already palmed his Remington, and Matt had unlimbered his Tranters, now seemed to be as good a time as any to start using them.

Sam threw himself down behind a water butt and fired hastily around one edge. There was no immediate cover on the other side of the street for Matt, so he just kept going with bullets chasing his heels until he crashed through the closed double doors of Brady's Saloon.

A bullet thunked into the other side of the water butt and Sam flinched and swore. As water began to cascade out through the splintery bullet-hole, he came around the side of the barrel and fired another shot. The horses up at the rack were stamping and shifting in their desire to break free and run, and Frank Wilson wasn't helping their nerves any because he was firing a weapon himself now, even though he was a sitting duck up there in the saddle.

A window smashed. Sam glanced sideways and saw Matt's face and gun-arm appear briefly in the star-shaped crack. A spear of flame lanced out of the Tranter's barrel and on the other side of the street Frank Wilson howled, hunched up and grabbed his chest.

For a moment Sam thought the man was out of the fight, but then he recovered and punched his handgun out to arm's-length again.

The stretch outside the marshal's office was a riot of activity now, as Wheelahan, Carson and the silent halfbreed, Denver Tree, ran for their horses. Sam and Matt were spoilt for targets, but because the light was so unsure and everyone out there was moving so fast, it was kind of hard to score.

Sam came up *over* the barrel this time, snap-aimed and shot Frank Wilson again. Wilson toppled sideways, his hat tumbling off to reveal his long, dark hair. He fell from the saddle like coffee from a pot, his limbs all loose and watery. He hit the ground hard and the horses started mincing sideways so that they wouldn't be anywhere near him.

Dan Wheelahan fired another hasty shot at the front of Brady's Saloon and his bullet tore needles of wood out of one door. Then he ran for the horses, tore his reins loose and hurled himself up into the saddle.

Sam came around the butt and fired at him but missed. In the same moment Denver Tree brought up his Le Mat, a vicious weapon that held nine shots instead of the usual six, and also packed an additional punch in the shape of an extra, centralised shotgun barrel that fired a charge of .20-bore buckshot.

It was the shotgun barrel that Tree used now – and when the charge of buckshot hit the butt, the butt virtually disintegrated.

Sam threw himself backwards, away from the exploding barrel. He hit the ground on his back and launched into a wild roll that took him into the mouth of a shadowy alley between one building and the next.

By then, Wheelahan's horse had trotted into the centre of the street, and Wheelahan himself was yanking hard on the reins to get the animal turned around and out of there. Matt fired at him just as he swung sideways on and hit the horse instead: the animal collapsed onto its forelegs with a hideous cough-scream.

Wheelahan kicked out of the stirrups, yelling curses. He threw himself out of the saddle and ran back to the hitch-rack, where Denver Tree and Emmett Carson were now getting themselves mounted and ready to ride.

Under any other circumstances, Wheelahan would have made straight for the spare horse they'd fetched along for the man they'd been hoping to bust out of jail, but Frank Wilson's mount was closer so he went for that one instead. He tore the reins from the rack, frantic and clumsy in his haste, then leapt up across leather.

As he and his men lit out in a receding thunder of gunfire, Sam dashed out into the street and emptied his .44 after them. A couple of answering shots blasted back at him out of the darkness, but they missed by a country mile.

After that there was only the moaning of the wind, and the scared whinnying of the shot and dying horse.

The saloon door opened and Matt came straight out and shot the horse in the head to put it out of its misery. His face was hard and morose. The death of the horse meant far more to him than the death of Lije

Tucker and Frank Wilson. They'd had it coming. The horse hadn't.

The owner of Brady's Saloon, not surprisingly named Brady, came out into the street and, once he was sure that Wheelahan and his men had gone, started to complain about the damage they'd done to his property.

Ignoring him, Sam and Matt went into the office. In their search for the key to Tom Powell's cell, Wheelahan and his friends had turned the place into a shambles.

Sam went through to the cellblock, reloading the .44 as he went. It was a long, cold room built from pitted stone blocks that had been painted grey. A narrow walkway ran down between four cells, two on either side.

Tom Powell was clutching the bars of the furthest cell on the right. As Sam had suspected, the bars had been polished to a bright and totally impractical shine.

Now, as Sam filled the doorway, the tall, sharp-faced woman-killer could not hide his sense of mortification.

Sam walked down the aisle towards him and Tom backed warily away from the bars. Sam put his Remington away and checked the lock. It was still intact. He brought his bleak grey eyes up onto the prisoner but said nothing.

A moment later he turned on his heel and went back outside. Matt was setting chairs back onto their legs and generally trying to clear the place up a bit. Sam went right on through and back into the street.

Now that the fire down at the municipal hall was all but out, the crowd had transferred to this end of town. As Sam came outside, Rance pushed through the mob and hustled over, breaking stride a little when his tired blue eyes snagged first on the dead horse and then on the dead man.

'Jee-sus Christ, Judge! What the hell happened?'

Sam hooked a thumb over one shoulder. 'Matt's inside. He'll tell you.'

Rance brushed past him. Sam glanced

down at Frank Wilson. Already ice was forming on the dead man's eyelashes, and the blood spattered across his body was crystallising.

He turned to face the muttering crowd. He saw Judge Moffat standing there in the forefront, his round face a picture of shock and horror. Then there was Brady, still complaining about the damage to his saloon, and Bob Robbins, Allen Nordyke, Al Braden, Braden's skinny friend Zack and John Miller.

He spotted the face he'd been searching for then, and went right after him. Alvin Clark saw him coming and tried to lose himself in the crowd, but the press of people was pretty thick by this time and he couldn't get away fast enough.

Sam reached out, grabbed him by one arm and yanked him back towards the office.

Clark put up a struggle and said indignantly, 'What do you think you're doing, man? Let go of me at once!'

Sam made no reply, just dragged him past

the horse and the dead man, up across the planking and into the office.

Inside, he threw Clark across the littery room and the attorney stumbled and came up against the far wall with a thump. Matt and Rance turned around as they made their entrance, and as Sam went over and grabbed Clark by the lapels of his hastily-donned jacket, Judge Moffat and Bob Robbins came through the door to join them.

'What's going on here?' demanded Rance.

Sam gave Clark a shake. 'You told 'em, didn't you?' he said.

Clark shook his head desperately. 'I don't know what you're *talking* about! I demand–'

'You told 'em you didn't think you stood a chance in hell of gettin' Tom Powell off that murder charge,' Sam snarled. 'Then you told 'em how we was figurin' to try him tomorrow. That's why they tried to bust him out of here tonight, isn't it?'

Clark looked imploringly at Rance. 'Are you going to let this man–'

Rance said, 'Is it true, what Judge is saying?'

'Of course it isn't true!'

'You're a damned liar, Clark,' Sam hissed. 'I saw you gabbin' with 'em earlier on, over at Brady's.' Bluffing, he added, 'I was right there at the next table. I heard every word.'

Clark's shoulders fell and he looked like he was going to pass out. 'They … asked me how I thought the … the case was going to go,' he sobbed. 'I … t-told them.' His head snapped up suddenly. 'But I had no idea what they were planning to do, I swear!'

Rance took off his hat and ran splayed fingers up through his hair. 'Damn you, Clark!' he said.

'Do you really think I had any choice, against men like that?' Clark snapped miserably. 'You tell them everything they want to know, or else—'

He broke off and shuddered.

Silence poured into the office. Rance looked from Sam to Matt, from Matt to Judge Moffat, from Judge Moffat to Bob Robbins. Finally he said, 'I'm sick at the sight of you, Clark. Get out of here. But don't you *dare* try to leave town. You've got a case to defend in the morning.'

Clark's surprise wiped all the other emotions off his face. 'But … the municipal hall…?'

'Thanks to Dan Wheelahan, the municipal hall's only fit for levelling now,' Rance said. 'But we'll find someplace else in time for tomorrow.' He fixed the attorney with a burning look. 'The trial's going ahead as planned, Clark. You hear me? By this time tomorrow, all the evidence will have been heard and the jury have reached its verdict. One way or another, tomorrow is Judgment Day.'

The Texans left Rance to arrange for the street to be cleared and started down towards their hotel. It was late and the air stank of burnt timber. But there was still the matter of Eve Tucker to attend to.

'*Sam! Sam!*'

Startled, they looked around. Hurrying

down towards them on the other side of the road was Alice, waving frantically to attract their attention.

With a muttered, 'Go on ahead,' to Matt, Sam crossed over to meet her, and when he was within reach, she threw her arms around him and held him tight, much to his surprise and extreme discomfiture.

'Oh God, Sam! Thank God you're all right!' she said, all teary-eyed. 'I saw the fire, of course, and came down to see if there was anything I could do to help, but then, when they said that you'd been involved in a gunfight...' She broke off and stepped back to inspect him. 'You're all right? You're *sure* you're all right?'

He smiled. 'I'm fine,' he replied. 'But Rance's just about as mad as a wet hen.' She frowned and he explained exactly what had happened, and why.

They heard footsteps behind them then, and turned around just as Matt trotted up. As Matt tipped his hat to Alice, Sam said, 'The Tucker woman all trussed up an' ready for jail?'

'She came to and lit out.'

Sam growled irritably. 'An' no-one tried to stop her?'

'No-one was *there* to stop her. They were all down at the municipal hall, or–'

Alice frowned some more. 'The Tucker woman? You mean Eve Tucker?'

Matt said yes, Eve Tucker, and told her all about the attempt on his life.

'Good heavens! How terrible, Mr Dury! Whatever is this town coming to?'

'Well, it's like you said earlier,' Sam reminded her. 'Once this business is behind us, life'll get back to normal.' He cleared his throat and offered his arm. 'May I walk you home, ma'am?'

'Oh, I really, I–'

He raised his hand. 'Come on, now. It's too late for a woman to be out all by her lonesome, anyway.' He looked at Matt, who swiftly hid a bemused smile. 'Think you can stay outta trouble till I get back, Matthew?'

Matt shrugged and said seriously, 'I'll sure

try – *Samuel.*'

'You do that. Come on, Alice.'

Matt watched them walk away, arm in arm. They made a handsome pair. Then he glanced up at the hotel and thought about Eve Tucker. He wondered if she'd try anything else against him. He hoped not – for he purely hated fighting hellcats.

Sam and Alice ambled slowly up the gentle, timbered hill and left the town behind them. What with one thing and another, it had been a hell of a night, and from the way Alice held onto his arm and gave it a little squeeze every so often, Sam had a notion that it was nowhere near finished yet.

They reached her place and she asked him if he wanted to come inside for a cup of coffee. He confessed that he *was* feeling a mite parched, and followed her into the darkened cabin.

They fumbled their way down the short hallway and through the homely parlour, where orange embers glowed invitingly in the fireplace and cast the faintest light to illuminate their passage. Mitzi stirred briefly in her blankets and meowed a soft greeting.

The kitchen was square and functional. Alice led the way and reached up to the central lamp, all fingers and thumbs as she tried to get it lit. Sam paused a moment in the doorway, watching her. When it became obvious that she was having trouble raising the funnel, he said, 'Here, let me.'

He went over. They were as close now as they'd been earlier, and just like earlier, he still wanted to kiss her very much. He looked down at her through the shadows. Moonlight shafted in through the window and chased her face with silver.

She came into his arms and they kissed gently. Then she closed her own arms around him and a string of little, exploratory kisses became something longer, stronger and more meaningful.

For some time the dark house was filled only with their heavy breathing and a few odd, affectionate whisperings. Then they broke apart, and without looking at him, Alice said, 'Do you *have* to go back to town tonight, Sam?'

Sam opened his mouth to say no, but before he could speak he heard a floorboard creak behind him. Alice heard it too, and she sucked in a deep, startled breath.

Sam tried to disentangle himself from her and spin around. A big man came at him from out of nowhere, one arm raised. Sam said something, Lord knew what, and got a brief glimpse of moonlight dribbling off the barrel of a handgun.

He brought one arm up to ward off the blow, but he was too slow. The pistol struck him alongside the head and he groaned and winced and his legs started to fold up beneath him.

Alice cried out, '*Sam!*'

Her voice came to him from the far end of a long, long tunnel. *Sam, sam, sam, sam…*

The man hit him again. Alice tried to scream, but someone muffled it with a palm. Sam fell flat on his face, fighting to cling to consciousness. Someone kicked him and he curled up.

A gun was cocked. A man's voice said, 'Not another sound, Mrs Colbert.'

Just before Sam blacked out completely, he thought with despair, *Aw Christ, it's Dan Wheelahan.*

Dan Wheelahan's got us.

Too keyed-up to sleep for very long, Rance was up again just before daybreak and rattling the doors of Brady's Saloon.

There was no instant response. Brady, a small, dapper man with a pinched face and artificially-coloured hair, tended to sleep late, and it was rare indeed to see him up before nine in the morning, a time which most other folks considered to be somewhere around the middle of the working day.

Undaunted, Rance kept rattling the doors until finally he heard a voice coming distantly from the other side of the bullet-scarred entrance. 'All right, all right! Just … just give me a minute, will you?'

Slowly Brady unbolted, unlocked and finally opened the door. When he saw the lawman standing there, he sniffed suspiciously. 'Oh,' he said. 'It's you.' In the next moment he brightened. 'You come to compensate me for all this damage, Colbert? I warn you, glass don't come cheap in this neck of the woods. I got to import it all the way—'

'I want you to clear your place and get it swept out,' Rance broke in. 'Then I want you to set your tables and chairs out just the way we had 'em set out down at the hall.'

Brady squinted his dark, sleep-puffed eyes. He looked ludicrous in his red combinations and thick, plum-coloured dressing-gown. *What?*

'We're holding Tom Powell's trial here today,' explained Rance.

'Here? *Oh* no. You can think again, marshal.'

'Don't fight me on this, Brady. You can't. I'm using the authority vested in me to requisition your premises.'

Brady said, 'The hell with your authority! You think I want this place going up in smoke the way the municipal hall did last night? I don't want anything to *do* with it!'

Rance let him have his say. Around him dawn was slowly filtering through the clustered grey clouds. 'Court convenes at nine o'clock sharp,' he said. 'And if this place isn't ready for it, I might just decide to take a closer look at those rigged games I hear you've been running lately.'

Brady glanced away from him. 'What's that supposed to mean?'

'You know damn' well what it means,' Rance replied. 'Just see to it.'

He turned and strode away. Up at the far end of town the municipal hall stood in silence, partially eaten away at the rear and scarred by ugly black fire-smudges. Along the street, storekeepers were preparing for a new day's trading, setting out boxes and barrels or sweeping the light dusting of snow and ice down into the road. Eateries were firing up in readiness for the breakfast crowd, and the smell of frying bacon and spitting eggs made his stomach groan.

He went into the first restaurant he came to, ate breakfast and asked the waitress to pass the word that the Powell trial would be starting down at Brady's Saloon at nine o'clock.

He repeated the same message to every storekeeper and townsman he passed on his subsequent patrol of town, then found and told Judge Moffat, Bob Robbins and Alvin Clark, as well.

The sun did its best to break through, but it was an uphill struggle. It looked as if it was going to be another cold, windy day. Matt came in at around eight o'clock and said, 'Whole town's buzzing with the news, Rance. You think Brady's place'll be big enough to hold all the folks who plan to attend?'

Rance smiled wearily. 'That place is packed to the rafters most nights. You'd be surprised how many people Brady can pack in.'

Brady himself came over ten minutes later. 'We've run out of chairs,' he said sourly.

Rance nodded. 'No problem. There's plenty we can salvage from the hall. Matt – take Brady and his hired men down there and see what you can fetch back.'

Matt nodded and started for the door. 'Yo.'

Eight-thirty rolled around. People began to head for the saloon – not that it looked much like a saloon any more. Brady and his employees had cleared the floor and set the furniture out in roughly the same manner that they'd seen at the municipal hall. Already Bob Robbins and Alvin Clark were at their respective tables, consulting their notes, while Judge Moffat was out back, inspecting Brady's small, cluttered office with some distaste.

At eight-fifty Rance unlocked Tom Powell's cell, cuffed his hands behind his back and shoved him across the street. Tom went slowly and in silence, his dead-eyed expression giving nothing away.

Most all of Little Cody was packed into the saloon. The buzz of conversation died down as Rance and the defendant came in and Matt closed the doors behind them. The muttering started up all over again as Rance cuffed Tom to his chair and then stood back to scan the crowd.

After a moment, he raised one hand and gestured for Matt to come and join him.

When he was near enough, Rance said in a lowered voice, 'I don't see my mother or Mr Judge anywhere, Matt. Have you seen them this morning?'

Matt looked at the crowd himself, then shook his head. Rance's question put him in something of a quandary. How did you tell a man that your partner had most likely spent the night with his mother? And that was certainly what must have happened, since Sam hadn't returned to the hotel after seeing Alice back to her cabin.

But now that Rance mentioned it, he began to feel uneasy. There was no way that Sam or Mrs Colbert would miss the trial.

And he doubted that they would be so indiscreet as to arrive late or not at all.

Looking into Rance's worried eyes was like seeing his own misgivings thrown back at him through a mirror. 'Want me to go see if I can round 'em up?' he asked quietly.

Rance bobbed his head. 'I'd appreciate it.'

Matt turned away and left at a hurried walk.

Five minutes later Judge Moffat came out of Brady's office and Rance called for the court to rise. The judge shuffled across to his desk, sat down and struck his gavel three times, bringing the court to order.

It was exactly nine o'clock.

Matt stood outside Alice Colbert's cabin and banged on the door a third time. Still there was no answer.

He stood back, agitated and apprehensive now, then bent to peer in through the windows. He could see nothing through the gathered lace and swore irritably. He returned to the door, rapped his knuckles against it again, then stood back. Still nothing.

Right. If he was mistaken about this, he'd apologise and make good the damage. If he *wasn't...*

He raised one booted foot and kicked at the handle. The door splintered inwards at his second kick, and he followed it in with a gun in his hand, fearing the worst.

The cabin was silent and cold. Matt went into the parlour. It was empty. He called Mrs Colbert's name. There was no response. He called Sam's name. Nothing.

What the *hell* had happened to them after they'd left him the previous night?

Something touched his legs and he twisted around with the Tranter cocked and ready for shooting.

Mitzi looked up at him, meowed and then rubbed up against his legs again.

Relaxing, he let the hammer down and bent to stroke the hungry cat. If Sam and Alice had made it this far, Mitzi must have seen what had happened to them. 'Too bad you can't talk and tell me,' he murmured.

He continued his search of the house. The bedroom was empty. The bed hadn't been slept in. The kitchen was similarly deserted … until he found five dark red patches in the centre of the floor.

Dried blood.

Matt swallowed hard. He called for Mrs Colbert again, not really expecting a reply this time, then started back into the parlour.

If it hadn't been for a stray draught stealing in through the open front door and blowing a scrap of paper off the dining table and onto the floor, Matt might not have discovered it at all until much later.

As it was, the crumpled white square stood out clearly against the coloured swirls of the carpet, and he went directly over and picked it up.

His lips worked soundlessly as he read what had been printed on it in pencil. He had to read it through twice before it really sank in. Then–

'*Oh, Jesus,*' he whispered, looking out the

window at the snowy, timbered ranges that stretched away towards the higher mountains. 'God help you if you've harmed them, Wheelahan.'

NINE

'*Oooh...*'

Sam screwed his eyes tight shut against the light slanting in through the small, high window and rolled slowly onto his side to get away from it. Half the Indian nation was banging war drums inside his skull, and he felt like hell.

'Sam! Sam ... are you all right? Oh, thank God, I was so frightened...'

He felt hands on him, trying to roll him onto his back, and still disoriented, he tried to resist them. Then something inside his brain identified the voice as belonging to a woman – Alice – and the picture he got of her in his mind triggered another memory – of what had happened in her kitchen the previous night.

He groaned again. He'd been pistol-whipped. No wonder he felt like hell. Briefly he must have regained consciousness, because he remembered being slung across a saddle, the horn stabbing into his side, a smell of perfume that told him that Alice was sharing the saddle with him.

He cracked his eyes open again and tried to sit up. The light hurt him, but from the look of it he gauged the time to be somewhere about six or seven in the morning. He'd been out for better than seven hours, then.

Alice helped him up and when he had his back against a grain sack, he sucked in a long, deep breath to quell his nausea.

After a moment he focused on her. She was kneeling beside him, her wheat-coloured hair bedraggled, her face pale and cold-looking, her eyes a little bloodshot from earlier tears. He reached out one arm and she came into his comforting embrace.

'Oh, Sam … those *wicked* men!'

'There, there…'

It didn't take much figuring out, what had

happened. He'd already guessed that Wheelahan had decided to bust Cousin Tom out of jail because he knew the man was sure to be found guilty and sentenced to hang. When that had failed, he must have settled on a different plan – to guarantee Tom's release by holding Alice as a hostage.

Well, it had been Wheelahan's lucky night after all, because he'd ended up with two hostages instead of one.

At last he thought to look around them. They were in a small, airless storage shed somewhere. There were a few old paint pots sitting on a shelf, some sacks of feed, a few cartons filled with airtights, a stack of barrels. The place was dirty, and stank of cold and damp.

'You all right?' he croaked, beginning to feel a little better now that the thumping in his head was starting to subside.

'Yes, Sam.'

He nodded to the door. 'Bolted?'

'There's a little give in it,' she said. 'But I think it's been padlocked from the outside.'

He untangled himself from her and got to his feet. They'd taken his Remington, but not his few remaining cigars. That, he thought, was some consolation. But only when he'd settled one in the corner of his mouth did he realise they'd also taken his matches.

'Aw...'

He stuffed the cigar back into his shirt pocket, dragged a couple of cartons over to the window and climbed up onto them. The single window was set so high up in the wall that it was the only way he could reach it.

Hoisting himself up, he peered outside. He saw a backyard with chickens pecking at scraps and a couple of old hounds chained to a roughly-built dog-house. About thirty yards away a big, sturdy-looking structure was all but buried beneath a thick mantle of snow. The Powell roadhouse? Sam didn't think it could be anyplace else.

He was just about to climb down again when the back door opened and a massive little woman lumbered outside. She had a hard, round face that was flushed red from working in the kitchen, and thick arms. The cold wind ruffled her fine grey hair, so that it stood up on her head like the fuzz of a dandelion. She bent, caught one of the chickens in her big, calloused hands, then straightened up again and snapped the fowl's neck without missing a beat.

She turned and took the bird, still fluttering limply in its death-throes, back into the kitchen and closed the door.

Sam raised one eyebrow and muttered, 'Charmin'.'

He climbed down off the cartons and went over to the door. Alice was right beside him. Somehow they had to get out of here. But without horses, and in these conditions, how far could they expect to get?

'*Dammit!*' said Rance. 'I should've let the miners lynch Tom when they wanted to!'

He started for the door, then pulled up sharp when Judge Moffat barred his way. 'Wait a minute, Rance! Just where do you think you're going?'

Rance's face was a promise of murder. 'I'm getting a posse together and getting my mother back,' he replied. 'Mr Judge, too. And I'll kill anyone who gets in my way.' He made to push past. 'I figure they're holding them out at the roadhouse. They must be. Anyplace closer would be too chancy.'

Bob Robbins said, 'But *think* a minute, man! This fellow Wheelahan is as good as holding a gun to your mother's head! If you race out there in the mood you're in now, you might well scare him into pulling the trigger!'

'Then I'll go alone, quietly, approach the place from a different direction–'

'Either way, you'd still be taking a terrible risk,' Lew Moffat opined. 'Now, when we've got your mother and Mr Judge back safe and sound...'

'That's your answer then, is it? Say to hell with the law and let Tom walk free?'

Rance turned away from them. The trial had been well underway by the time Matt had let himself back into the saloon and told him the news. From there Rance had approached the bench, and following more whispers the judge had announced that court would break for one hour, and convene again at ten-thirty. After that, he, Robbins and Clark had joined Rance and Matt here in the cramped, dingy confines of Brady's office.

Now Rance went over to Brady's desk, picked up the note that Matt had found out at his mother's place and read it through again. IF OURS GOES FREE, YOURS GO FREE. Not for the first time he told himself that Wheelahan was a clever bastard. He'd mentioned no names. As evidence, it would prove nothing. And even if his mother and Mr Judge later testified to their abduction, where would that get them? Another trial? Go through all of this *again?*

It was now twenty after ten. Already he could hear the townsfolk coming back into the saloon outside and finding their seats.

He felt the others watching him, waiting. He felt pressured and out of his depth. He had to reach a decision. Reach it, and then live with it. But what decision should he make?

He owed something to his mother and Mr Judge – that went without saying. But he also owed something to the parents of Maureen Randall, the murdered girl. And to his badge, too.

It was an impossible decision to make, and yet he must make it. Somehow.

The life went out of him and he sank down onto the edge of the desk. He looked at Matt and said, piteously, *'Help* me.'

Matt nodded slowly. 'I'll help you,' he replied softly.

Then he set about telling them what they were going to do.

Alice was right. The door had been pad-locked from the outside. They managed to shove it open about six inches, and then the chain yanked tight and that was that.

Sam got his fingertips around the edge of the door and pulled it shut again to keep out

274

the worst of the wind. There was no way either of them could squeeze through that kind of gap, and so far they'd turned up nothing they could use as a lever to widen it any further.

Sam's eyes returned to the high, small window. At a pinch he figured they could both slip out that way. But how could he smash the window without their captors hearing it?

He wanted to swear, but mindful of Alice's presence, he kept quiet and tried to use his brain more constructively.

They were about fifteen miles from town. Without horses, and in this weather, that might just as well be fifteen *times* fifteen. Any way you looked at it, they'd have to get horses once they got out of this shed.

Alice was watching him worriedly. He looked at her, shivering in the cold, and tried to smile, but the gesture made the healing gash up on the right side of his head tug a bit. He went back across to the door, shoved it open again, reached through and grabbed hold of the chain. It was so cold that his palm nearly stuck to it, and he yelped in pained surprise.

'*Sam!*'

'It's all right … all r–'

Suddenly he stiffened.

In a whisper Alice said, 'What is it?'

Hurriedly he tugged the door shut again, then turned and pushed her down to the far end of the small shed. 'Someone's comin',' he answered in an undertone. 'Sit down, quick!'

Confused, she said, 'What about you?'

He threw himself down on the ground, reawakening fresh pain in his head. 'I ain't come to yet, Alice.'

He turned onto his side and closed his eyes. Now Alice heard footsteps coming closer, making little shushing noises as they flattened the snow underfoot. A moment later she heard someone breathing; a key turning in the padlock: the jingle of the chain sliding loose.

The door opened.

Sam tried to breathe deep and slow. He felt the newcomer studying him for a long time. Finally the man kicked one of his feet. Sam rocked gently, forcing his muscles to stay loose. Above him a man said, 'Ain't your lover-boy come round yet?'

There was a pause as Alice fought to get the words out. 'No. I … I'm worried about him. I think you hit him too hard last night.'

'I brought you some eats,' said the voice. It was the voice of a youngish man, not Wheelahan, probably not Denver Tree, but possibly Emmet Carson. Sam pulled in another deep breath and kept his ears attuned so he could pinpoint the man's approximate whereabouts.

'Here,' said the voice.

Sam smelled bacon and burnt grease.

Alice took the plate and set it aside. She wasn't hungry and no-one could blame her. Carson said, 'Cheer up, lady. Your son likely knows what happened to you by this time. Soon as he lets the Powells' boy go, you'll be released.'

'How do I know that?' demanded Alice.

Sam heard the smile in Carson's reply. 'You don't.' He grunted as he crouched beside her. 'But I tell you what I'll do. You show me a little … consideration … an' I'll make sure no-one hurts you.'

Alice caught her breath. 'What … what do you mean, "consideration"?'

'Oh, you know.' He paused meaningfully. 'A little lovin'.'

He reached for her and she tried to push him away, but he forced himself upon her, and after that there were some muffled, animal-like sounds as he kissed her.

Carson pushed her back and ran his rough hands across the soft material of her dress. Alice said breathlessly, 'Please… Oh, please, I beg you–!'

'Come on now, while we still got the chance…'

Further protestations were choked off as Carson stole another kiss.

Sam forced himself to hold back a moment longer. Then, when he could stand it no more, he opened his eyes and turned his head oh-so-gently. Emmett Carson was using his weight to pin Alice down on the grain sacks, and was covering her face with wet kisses. His hat had fallen off and Sam could clearly see the bald patch at his crown.

The man's fevered breathing was hideous. Sam could hardly stomach to hear it. And there was no longer any reason why he should.

He rolled over, came up in a crouch and lunged at the hardcase. Carson was carried away and his reflexes were slow. It was only when Sam grabbed him – one hand twisted into his hair, the other twisted into his jacket – that he suddenly came down to earth and opened his mouth to cry out.

By then, however, it was way too late.

Sam lifted him off Alice and drove him forward so that his face smashed into one of the barrels that were stacked there. The impact made a heavy thunking sound and Sam did it twice more, moving hard and fast, to make his point.

He let Carson fall then, and the man rolled off Alice with blood still squirting from his pulped nose.

As Alice slipped out from under him, a fist to her mouth to stifle a scream, Sam grabbed one of the paint pots down off the shelf and swung it in a wide arc.

It slammed Carson's face sideways and his muddy brown eyes rolled up into his head. Sam tossed the pot aside, yanked the man's Smith & Wesson .45 from its holster and rammed it into his own pouch, then grabbed Alice by one hand and pulled her across to the door.

The yard was quiet but for the pecking chickens. Cautiously he stepped outside, with Alice at his heels. It was bitter out there, but neither of them felt the cold. Sam scanned the area. Everything seemed quiet.

What they really needed, he told himself, was a plan. But there was no time for that. All they could do now was try to skirt around the roadhouse, get into the stable on the other side of the trail, help themselves to a couple of horses and then get the hell out of there.

Drawing in an icy breath, he peeled away from the shed and Alice came after him, lifting her skirt a bit in order to run faster. They cut across the yard, heading for the corner of the roadhouse, eyes fixed on the closed back door, willing it to remain shut.

They got about halfway across the yard and then the hounds sprang up and started barking and straining at their chains, and Alice hissed, 'Dammit!'

Sam could only agree with the sentiment. Now that those blasted dogs had started yapping, their escape was sure to be discovered.

Alice stumbled and cried out, but Sam kept ploughing forwards, dragging her along with him. They reached the corner and tore around it, churning snow up around their driving feet. The barking grew muffled, and the frantic sawing of their breathing took its place.

They made it along the side wall, hesitated

only briefly and then plunged on across the wrinkled trail, heading for the stable. Somewhere behind them the roadhouse door swung open and shouts filled the air. Alice cried out again but still Sam kept hauling her on towards the stable. He had a gun. At least in the stable he might be able to hold them off for a while.

Dimly he realised that someone was racing towards him from behind and to the right. He tried to outrun the man but he was getting too old and he just didn't have it in him any more. Whoever it was crashed into him and the air pushed out of him in a debilitating rush. Arms went around his legs and he went down in a tangle, burning his palms on the snow.

He rolled onto his back, saw Jed Powell getting his legs under him and preparing to leap at him again. With a roar, Sam brought one boot up and kicked the man right in the balls, and Jed screamed and twisted away.

There was more yelling as Nathan Powell, 'Becca, Eve and Saul – now nursing his wounded shoulder in a sling – came chasing out onto the trail. It was deafening. Sam struggled up, reached for the .45. Then another man – Denver Tree – came racing out of the roadhouse, kicked the weapon from his hand and then kicked him, too.

Alice screamed, but the halfbreed only shoved her aside and went on kicking Sam again and again, and neither did her frenzied protestations stop Jed Powell from climbing back to his feet and joining in.

With no way to fight back, Sam could only hunch up under the onslaught and try to stay conscious until it was finished. But it just went on and on and on, and so did Alice's screams and the yelling of the blood-hungry Powells, until unconsciousness drowned him in a funereal black tide.

Alice knelt over him, trying her best to protect him from further harm, but Jed only pushed her aside and kicked Sam some more, until finally Dan Wheelahan shouldered through the ring of onlookers and pulled him off.

'All right, all right – that's *enough!*'

It fell quiet then, under the blazing strength of his gaze.

He looked down at Sam. Sam lay unmoving. Blood, diluted by the watery snow, stained the ground around him, looking like little red roses.

Then he looked at Alice. 'Emmett's dead,' he said, almost gently. 'Your man killed Emmett, Mrs Colbert.'

He kicked Sam himself for that.

'Please…' Alice begged, holding onto the man from Texas. 'Don't hurt him any more…'

Wheelahan looked at her as the wind picked up and tugged at the brim of his Jeff Davis hat. At last he spun away and said, 'She's right. If we kill him, the law'll be down on us for sure. Lock 'em back up, then fetch some shovels. Best we bury Emmett before the snow comes again.'

Jed rubbed at his sore crotch. 'What about me?' he complained. 'You can't expect *me* to do no diggin'.'

Wheelahan glanced at him. 'Grab your rifle and trek out to yonder pass, then,' he barked. 'You can keep a look-out for when your brother comes ridin' home.'

The prisoner was brought back over to the saloon and cuffed to his chair. At ten-thirty Judge Moffat called the court to order and when silence settled over the big, sawdusted room he spoke.

'It's cold and I daresay you good people have got better things to do, so I'll come straight to the point. I find what I am about to say frankly unpalatable, but in the circumstances I have little choice in the matter.

'Tom Powell, your kinsmen have fought a long and dirty campaign to force this court to drop the charges against you, a campaign which has culminated in the abduction of two people, Marshal Colbert's mother and Mr Sam Judge.'

A buzz rose up from the scandalised townspeople, but the judge ignored it and carried on. 'Now, there are all kinds of things we *could* do in this situation. But your family has an unenviable reputation for murder, and we're not prepared to take any chances with the people they're holding.

'Therefore, we have chosen to disregard all of the impossible options we've just spent the last hour or so discussing, and go for the only course of action that is truly open to us – may the Good Lord forgive us.'

Judge Moffat took off his spectacles and pinched the flesh between his eyes, then said reluctantly, 'Tom Powell, it is the decision of this court...'

Morning gave way to early afternoon. The sky grew heavy and fresh snow started falling, adding to old drifts and building new ones.

Hunkered beside a meagre fire not all that far from where his brother-in-law had been killed a couple of days before, Jed Powell kept his shifty green eyes fixed on the narrow pass through which Tom would have to come if Cousin Dan's plan worked out and the authorities in Little Cody set him free.

The temperature dropped and the ache in Jed's groin transmitted itself up into his head as well. He was tired. And hungry. He had no patience for this look-out business. 'Far as he was concerned, it was a waste of time. He'd much sooner be back at the roadhouse, soaking up the warmth of a blazing log f–

Suddenly he twisted around. He'd caught the faint jingle of harness on the wind and, clutching his Winchester tighter, he peered forward cautiously through the screening brush and into the pass below.

Even though the snow had cut visibility, he could just about make out two riders some thirty yards distant. The riders halted at the mouth of the pass and exchanged a few words. A marshal's star flashed on the coat of one of the men, identifying him as Rance Colbert. In the next moment he recognised the other man by his hat and jacket.

Tom!

Colbert reached out and Tom shrugged

him off and gestured irritably for him to beat it back to town. Colbert said something else, then turned his horse away and heeled it away into the blizzard, leaving Tom to come ahead alone.

As he came through the pass, Jed left the shelter of the brush and slid slantwise down the incline to greet him. He could hardly believe that Dan's plan had actually worked! 'Course, Tom couldn't stay around these parts, not after this. He'd have to clear out of the country and take his crazy woman-killing ways with him. But at least he wouldn't end up dangling from the end of a rope.

Jed made it to the bottom of the slope at just the same moment that Tom gigged his prancing horse through the pass and came level with him. With a wave, Jed waded through the hip-high snow and yelled, 'Well, lookee what the wind's blown in!'

Tom shifted in the saddle and looked down at him. He had a gun in his hand.

The smile froze on Jed's countenance. He looked up into his brother's face … except that it wasn't his brother up there, even though he was rigged out in Tom's gear, and riding Tom's horse.

It was that feller who'd killed Lije. Matt Dury.

Jed said, '*What–?*'

Matt brought the pistol down in a flashing arc. The sight caught Jed in the mouth and threw him backwards into the snow. He cried out, released the Winchester and tried to push himself upright, but then Matt leapt from the saddle and landed on top of him. Matt grabbed him by his jacket and wrenched him over onto his back. Jed glared up at him and swore foully, his mouth mashed and bloody.

Matt shoved the barrel of his right-side Tranter into Jed's face and Jed shut up quick. He spoke quietly, with death in his bleak grey eyes. 'My partner and the woman,' he hissed. 'They still alive down there?'

Jed said, 'Go to–' Then the gun shoved harder into his face and, more cautiously, he nodded.

'Where're you keeping 'em?' Matt barked.

Jed's voice became a high squeak. 'Sh-shed! Out back!'

Matt nodded, took the Tranter away from Jed's face and brought it around in a short, violent crescent. Twice he clubbed the red-head, until he was certain that the man was unconscious.

He turned when he heard Rance heeling his sorrel down through the pass to join him, and together they dragged Jed back up the slope. Rance changed into the unconscious man's jacket and hat, then went to catch up his horse while Matt hauled him across to the fire, tied him tight and then threw a blanket they took from one of his saddlebags over him. After that, they led Jed's poorly-used horse down the slope and mounted up.

Squinting through the driving snow, Rance said worriedly, 'This had better work.'

Matt hauled his Winchester from its scabbard and jacked in a shell. 'We know our people's still alive,' he replied. 'We know that they're being kept out back someplace.

It's up to us to *make* it work.'

They heeled their horses into motion as the wind rocked them sideways in their appropriated saddles, both men riding with scarves tugged up across their faces and gloved fingers curled around the triggers of the Winchesters they held athwart their laps.

A mile further on they saw lights glowing in the little square windows of the road-house, and Matt glanced at his companion and said, 'Ready?'

Rance's narrowed eyes looked sick in the gloomy afternoon light. 'As ready as I'm likely to be,' he replied.

They rode on down the trail, tight in the belly, and reined in before the roadhouse. Then Rance lifted his Winchester and fired two shots into the leaden sky, and yelled in a fair imitation of Jed Powell, 'Hey! Look what the wind's blown in!'

Twenty seconds ticked by. Then they saw an indistinct figure appear, wipe a slot in one of the steamy windows and peer outside. Through the coiling, spiralling snow the men from Little Cody held their breath, waiting.

A moment later the roadhouse door creaked open and the Powells came out, stamping and huddled against the cold, Nathan and Saul, 'Becca and Eve, Wheelahan and Tree. A regular family reunion.

Matt looked at them above the rough line of his scarf. Saul danced a little jig and said, 'That you, Tom! By God, we did it, didn't we? Showed them townsfolk a thing or two!'

'Becca said, 'Light, boy. I got a stew cookin'.'

Matt's only reply was to turn to Tom's mount sideways on, so that his Winchester was pointed at the lined-up family.

The wind moaned. Something died in Nathan's restless green eyes, and he said quietly, 'Tom?'

Matt shook his head and said, 'Uh-huh.'

Beside him, Rance tugged down his scarf and said, 'Throw down your weapons, all of you. You're under arrest.'

There was an instant then, a split second

that lasted forever, when no-one moved or spoke, and nothing happened.

Rance said, 'I mean it. There's been enough violence over this business.'

At last it all became clear. Tom wasn't coming home. Not ever. The law was too big for these people to intimidate any more. And when Wheelahan and the Powells finally realised that, everything exploded at once.

With a snarl, Denver Tree dropped into a crouch and went for his Le Mat. Saul grabbed awkwardly for the .45 tucked into his belt and turned sideways on. The women started yelling, and old Nathan brought up the rifle he habitually carried in the crook of his arm.

The halfbreed's Le Mat marked him as the most dangerous man among them, so Matt swung his Winchester onto him first and shot him in the arm. Tree screeched and flipped over onto the snow, but he was still clutching and able to use the deadly weapon so Matt worked the lever and shot him again, and this time his contorted face burst apart in a crimson detonation.

Roaring his fury, Dan Wheelahan dodged back into the roadhouse, leaving the Powells to it. Saul fetched up his handgun and triggered a shot at Rance. Rance threw himself down off his side-hopping horse, stumbled, fell, came up and fired back at him with his long gun braced against one hip.

Eve flung herself towards Matt, her face twisted in a scream and her fingers hooked for gouging. Up on his horse, Matt saw her coming, quickly kicked one boot out of the stirrup and shoved her back and down onto her rump.

By that time Nathan had his rifle up and was shooting indiscriminately, and the horse beneath Matt made a kind of coughing sound and crashed sideways, hurling him to the ground. Lights popped in his head and he blinked rapidly to clear them. In the next moment snow showered up beside him and he saw Saul blasting away at him from a distance of twelve feet.

Gunfire and yelling pressed down on their

eardrums. Saul kept coming forward with the .45 jumping in his fist. Then Rance tracked and shot him once, and Saul corkscrewed himself into the snow with blood drizzling from a hole in his chest.

'Bastards!' yelled Nathan, pumping the lever of his rifle as spittle flecked his thick, wiskery lips. 'Bastards!'

Matt leapt up and hit him with the stock of his Winchester before he could cause further mayhem, and Nathan grunted and went down spitting teeth. Screaming herself hoarse, 'Becca tore her own gun from the pocket of her apron. But–

Stabbing his smoking long gun at her, Rance snarled, 'Don't you *dare*, Mrs Powell.'

'Becca's head snapped up and she glowered at him. The snow twisted and fell around her. After a moment she looked at the two dead men, the one dead horse, and her husband rolling around in the slush, clutching his face, at her daughter, struggling helplessly to extricate herself from the wet, clinging snow.

Swearing, she threw her gun down with so

much angry force that the snow swallowed it whole.

'You sonsabitches,' she muttered bitterly.

Matt shouldered past her and went into the kitchen. The back door was ajar. Beyond it he could see Wheelahan kicking through the snow to get to a shed on the far side of the backyard, and a pair of hounds yapping and leaping around at the ends of ice-encrusted chains.

He surged across the room, burst out into the yard and bellowed Wheelahan's name, and Wheelahan stumbled a bit, then spun around and clawed out his sidearm.

He fired two shots and Matt threw himself sideways as glass shattered above and behind him. Wheelahan's gun spat flame twice more. Then Matt brought the stock of his Winchester up to his cheek, snap-aimed and fired back.

His first shot missed, so he worked the lever and fired again, and on the other side of the yard Dan Wheelahan cried out like a woman and hunched up, grabbing himself.

Matt levered and fired once more, and the other man went up on his toes, flung his arms wide, dropped his pistol and keeled over into the snow.

Matt straightened up, drained by the action, then pushed himself away from the road-house and stumble-ran across the yard to the shed. The door was padlocked shut, but the butt of the Winchester made short work of that.

At last he wrenched the shed door open.

Sam was sprawled on his back up at the far end of the little storage room. Alice Colbert was cradling his head in her lap. The woman was sobbing, and Sam's face was puffed up and covered in blood.

Matt looked at him. He wasn't moving. He didn't even appear to be breathing.

The colour drained from his face. His lips formed the name *Sam*, but no sound came out to accompany it. Walking slowly into the shed he mouthed it again. *Sam*.

Sam just lay there, as still as death.

Sam didn't regain consciousness at all until it was all over. He had no awareness of the gunfight, their rescue or their subsequent slow wagon-ride back to town. For him there was only a silent, black immensity that lasted a full forty eight hours.

Then he woke up.

He woke up to find himself bare-ass naked but for a mesh of pads and bandages, in Alice Colbert's bed, with Alice herself dozing at his bedside, a length of fluffy knitting forgotten in her lap.

He lay still for a while. The room was warm and comfortable, a lifetime removed from the shed in which they were being held—

He sat up sharp then, and screwed his face up at the pain it stirred in every joint and muscle. 'Uhhnn…!'

That woke Alice, and just like a mother hen she leaned over him, put her hands on his bruised shoulders and forced him back against the pillows, tears sparkling in her eyes as she inspected him.

'Easy now, Sam, easy… You took a terrible beating, and you'll have to take it slowly for a while…'

The pillow felt cool against his sweated flesh. '*Now* you tell me,' he croaked. She fetched him a glass of water and helped him raise his head and drink. The room stopped spinning and his stomach growled hungrily.

Finally he said, 'Wh-what happened?' and she told him.

Once all that sank in, she said, 'Rance stopped by about an hour ago. The trial's over, Sam. The jury found Tom Powell guilty and Judge Moffat sentenced him to hang. They'll be transporting him to the territorial capital tomorrow.'

She wiped the moisture from his forehead. 'Matt says he'll be calling in to see you later this evening, by the way. I don't mind telling you, that boy has been extremely worried about you.'

Sam grinned, pleased to hear it.

'Now rest,' she told him. 'It's over, Sam.

All over. Tom's folks are locked up in jail. I think Judge Moffat is going to tell them to leave the territory – and I think they'll probably go, too. All you've got to concern yourself with now is recovering your strength and getting well again.'

He winced. 'I got a feelin' that might take quite a spell.'

'Do you think you could stand to let me look after you till spring thaw comes, then?'

He considered nodding, decided against it and just rasped, 'If you think you could stand to have me as a patient.'

His stomach growled again and she squeezed his hand and got up. 'I'll fetch you some broth.'

'Obliged to you, Alice.'

He called her name again as she reached the door, and when she turned back she saw that he was frowning. 'Alice,' he said. 'How's my cat been doin' while I been out of it?'

She came back over. 'Mitzi? Sam, I ... I got the doctor to take a look at her once he was through seeing to you,' she replied. 'He examined her and said it could be, well, one of two things.'

That sounded ominous. 'Oh?' he said guardedly.

She nodded. 'Yes. He said it could be *boy*-kittens … or it could be *girl*-kittens.'

Sam's punished face went blank. 'You … you m-mean…?'

With a laugh, Alice grabbed for his hands again. 'Yes, Sam. Mitzi's in the family way.'

Sam put his head back on the pillow, more relieved than he could say. 'Well, if that don't beat all!' he breathed.

Suddenly a look of alarm came over his face, and Alice stiffened. 'Sam! Are you all right?'

'All right?' he repeated. 'Alice, I just realised what you said. If Mitzi's gonna have kittens, that means I'm gonna be a gran'pappy!'

The publishers hope that this book has given you enjoyable reading. Large Print Books are especially designed to be as easy to see and hold as possible. If you wish a complete list of our books please ask at your local library or write directly to:

Dales Large Print Books
Magna House, Long Preston,
Skipton, North Yorkshire.
BD23 4ND

This Large Print Book, for people
who cannot read normal print,
is published under the auspices of
THE ULVERSCROFT FOUNDATION